SNOWBOUND

When Amy agrees to help famous cosmetic surgeon Ethan Stopes write his memoirs, she is expecting a few quiet days in the country. Instead she spends an eventful Christmas trapped in a lonely manor with Ethan, his ex-wife, and his two children — and falls in love . . . Amy discovers Ethan's secret, and passions flare as the snow deepens. Somehow, she must help the enigmatic surgeon finish his book before it is too late . . .

FAY CUNNINGHAM

◆

SNOWBOUND

Complete and Unabridged

LINFORD
Leicester

First published in Great Britain in 2011

First Linford Edition
published 2011

British Library CIP Data

Cunningham, Fay.
    Snowbound.- -(Linford romance library)
    1. Plastic surgeons- -Fiction.
    2. Autobiography- -Authorship- -Fiction.
    3. Romantic suspense novels.
    4. Large type books.
    I. Title II. Series
    823.9′2–dc22

    ISBN 978–1–44480–564–2

Published by
F. A. Thorpe (Publishing)
Anstey, Leicestershire

Set by Words & Graphics Ltd.
Anstey, Leicestershire
Printed and bound in Great Britain by
T. J. International Ltd., Padstow, Cornwall

This book is printed on acid-free paper

1

Amy stared nervously at the house, wishing she had never agreed to this assignment. Steely grey clouds had gathered overhead and it looked set for snow. The remains of last night's frost still glistened at the edges of the circular drive and the house, large and imposing, frowned back at her. The red brick, set in a herringbone pattern, looked centuries old, and the windows were small and dark. Strange, twisted chimneys poked up from a high-pitched roof, while the gables looked as if they might be a home for bats.

Altogether, not particularly inviting.

Amy had parked her little car next to a shiny black Mercedes on the drive, but she could see two more cars parked in an open barn, one of them a large four-wheel-drive vehicle. There was no knocker on the door, and a brass

pull-ring sent a sound like a peal of church bells resonating inside the house. Amy winced, afraid she might have set off some sort of alarm system.

The man who opened the door had a face like a thundercloud.

'Yes?'

'Amy Franklin,' she said, holding out her hand in what she considered a friendly gesture.

His hands didn't move from his sides. 'And you are selling what?'

'No.' She gave a nervous little giggle, hating herself for it. 'No. I've come to assist Dr Stopes with his autobiography.'

'You're the ghost writer.'

Annoyed now, Amy took a good, long look at the man standing in front of her. He was tall, and quite good looking in a sombre, brooding way, with thick black hair flecked with grey curling on to his collar, and dark brown eyes burning with annoyance. She had seen a photo of the surgeon, and he had short, dark hair, and laughter lines around his eyes.

2

This man must be the live-in personal assistant she had been told about. Perhaps Dr Stopes preferred a male PA.

Amy decided she wasn't going to take any nonsense from the paid help. Start as you mean to go on, her grandmother had told her. She pulled herself up to her full height of five feet two inches and did her best to stare him in the eye. 'I'm a professional writer, not a ghost, and I'd be pleased if you'd inform Dr Stopes that I've arrived. My suitcase is in my car.' She smiled sweetly at him. 'Perhaps you could arrange for it to be taken to my room.'

Just for a second a smile turned up the corner of his mouth and he looked almost human. 'I'll arrange that for you, Miss Franklin.' He turned his back on her. 'If you'd care to follow me.'

The entrance hall was enormous. A refectory table took up most of the space and Amy counted ten high-back chairs with rose-coloured velvet seats. She almost missed the grand piano tucked away in a dark corner. The

3

centrepiece was an ornate brick fire-place filled with cheerfully burning logs, the only cheerful thing about the place that she could see. The man led her into a book-lined study off the main hall, also with a glowing fire, and told her to take a seat. She dropped onto a scuffed leather sofa and took her first proper breath for what seemed like hours.

This wasn't at all what she had expected.

When her agent had telephoned and asked if she was interested in helping Dr Stopes with his autobiography, she had mixed feelings. She didn't entirely agree with cosmetic surgery. Dr Stopes was one of the most sought after cosmetic surgeons in the country, but also one of the most reclusive. He refused to give interviews or talk about his clients, even though it had been suggested that some of the top celebri-ties had been to him for help, including royalty. Now he had decided to write a book about his life, and she had been asked to help. What she hadn't expected

was having to live and work for almost a month in this mausoleum of a house.

When the door opened she was about to leap to her feet, until she saw it was the same man who had let her in.

'Perhaps we should start again, Miss Franklin. I'm sorry I had to keep you waiting but I had some domestic business to take care of.' He held out his hand. 'I'm Dr Ethan Stopes.'

Amy climbed warily to her feet. This couldn't be Dr Stopes — could it? She took the proffered hand, it wasn't in her nature to ignore it, and was shocked at the unexpected spark of electricity on contact. She looked down at her hand in surprise, and then raised her eyes to meet his.

Yes, it was the same person, she realised. The photo she had seen must have been taken years before. This man was older, in his early forties she would have thought, and a lot leaner than his younger self. The little laughter lines were still there, but she wondered now if they might be caused by pain rather

than laughter. Looking into his eyes she saw the dark brown irises were flecked with gold, and found herself sinking into their depth. She pulled back sharply. No wonder he had clients queuing to go under his knife. With those eyes, he was a dangerous man.

You've been caught before, Amy, she told herself sharply. Don't let it happen again.

'I'll get Cathy to show you to your room. Dinner is at seven, nothing formal.' He stopped as if he had run out of things to say. 'I hope your stay here will be pleasant.'

He opened the door and walked out of the room and Amy stared after him, not sure if she should follow him or wait for Cathy, whoever she was. She didn't have long to wait. A pretty girl with fair, curly hair and a turned up nose came bounding into the room with a big smile on her face.

'Your room's ready, Miss Franklin, and Nick has taken up your luggage. Shall I show you where to go?' She

didn't give Amy a chance to reply. 'I'm glad you're going to be staying here. It gets a bit lonely sometimes, even though I go home every weekend. Norfolk's lovely, but I miss home.'

'Whereabouts is home?' Amy asked, following the girl out of the study.

'Essex.' She laughed. 'I'm an Essex girl. My mum and dad used to run a little hotel, so I know all about making beds.'

'So what are you doing working here, Cathy?'

They were halfway up the curved staircase, and Cathy turned round. 'The doctor, he's my uncle, my mother's brother, and he needed a bit more help with the house. Not that he can't manage on his own, but it's a big house, and I needed a job.'

'How many people live here?'

Cathy led Amy along a panelled corridor. 'There's Angela, my uncle's personal assistant. She's been with uncle Ethan for ages and she sort of runs the house as well, and Mrs

Peacock comes in each day to cook. Uncle Ethan's friend from London is staying here over Christmas, and Celia stays if she brings the kids with her. She's Dr Stopes' ex. She'll be coming for Christmas.' Cathy stopped and threw open a door. 'This is your room.'

Amy stood for a minute, just looking. The room was in the eaves of the house, with a sloping ceiling and a dormer window overlooking the garden. And what a garden it was. A green lawn sloped down to a wood, and stone tubs holding little conifers flanked a paved terrace. She thought she could see a gleam of water through the trees and longed to get out there and explore.

'You've got an en suite of sorts,' Cathy said, bringing Amy back to the present. 'More like a cupboard with a bath. And there are fresh towels, and more blankets in case you get cold.' She grinned. 'It gets freezing of a night. There's no fireplace in here. But the water's hot, so you can have a bath when you want, and I'll put a hot-water

bottle in your bed each night.'

'Thank you,' Amy said. When Cathy had left, she explored her domain. Unexpectedly, the room was reasonably light due to the dormer window, but the walls were panelled in dark oak and the furniture, what there was of it, matched the dark and gloomy theme. The bed took up most of the space, a four-poster without the drapes. Big carved posts on each corner of the bed brushed the slope of the ceiling, but it looked comfortable, and the duvet felt as if it was stuffed with real down.

She wanted to lie on the bed and gaze out at the garden, but a look at her watch told her she only had half an hour to dinner, and she had a feeling it wouldn't go down well if she was late on her first day. Informal, Dr Stopes had said, but did that mean jeans, or a short dress rather than long? She decided to have a quick shower and think about it, but the big enamel bath, although spotlessly clean, didn't have a shower fitting, and one look at the size

of the tub told her it would probably take half an hour to fill. Plenty of hot water, Cathy had said, so an all-over wash would have to do.

She settled for a black woollen skirt and a long-sleeved sweater in amethyst jersey. The cold had begun to creep into her bones, and there was already a thin film of frost on the inside of her bedroom window, so she draped a black cardigan over her shoulders. She was going to have to ask for a heater of some sort otherwise she wouldn't last a week, let alone three. Thank goodness she wouldn't be here for long, and back home in her centrally heated flat before Christmas.

The hall was deserted, although the fire still glowed warmly in the hearth. She heard the sound of voices and eased open a door into what would probably be called a drawing room. She stood just outside the door for a moment, trying to place the people in the room. Dr Stopes stood in front of yet another fire, his elbow on the

mantelpiece, a glass in his hand. He looked incredibly handsome, Amy thought, like a gentleman from a Regency novel. By his side was a man of about the same age. He wasn't as tall as the doctor, and his hair was cut short, but he was equally attractive in his own way. He was carrying on an animated conversation with Ethan Stopes, waving his arms and nearly spilling the drink he held in his hand. Over by the window, a woman of about Amy's age was sitting by herself reading a book.

As Amy walked into the room all three heads turned towards her, and she felt like a specimen in a jar. 'Good evening,' she said, trying to sound nonchalant, 'I hope I'm not late.'

The younger of the two men, whom Amy assumed must be the friend from London, came towards her. 'Felix,' he said, bending to kiss her on the cheek. 'Felix Manning. And you must be Amy. Let me get you a drink.' He guided her towards a sideboard holding bottles and glasses. 'I think Ethan stocks most of

everything, so what can I get you?'

'A white wine spritzer would be nice, please.'

He raised a dark eyebrow and then studied the bottles. After a moment's thought, he poured wine from an opened bottle into a wine glass and handed it to her. 'Before I drown a really good wine with soda, just taste this for me and tell me what you think.'

He held the bottle so she couldn't see the label, but she took a sip and smiled at him. 'This is a really nice white Bordeaux, Sauvignon Blanc I would imagine, and I agree it's too good to drown. But I'm thirsty, so give me a less expensive wine with soda, or the Bordeaux and a glass of water.'

He threw back his head and laughed out loud. 'You've got a good one here, Ethan. She knows her wines.' He poured bottled water into a long glass. 'Get rid of the thirst first, and then enjoy the wine.'

Conscious that Dr Stopes was looking at her, and unable to manage

two glasses at the same time, she stood the wine glass back on the table and allowed Felix to lead her over to the fireplace. Ethan Stopes gave her a disinterested nod and then called across the room to the woman by the window. 'Where's my niece, Angela? That girl needs to eat.'

Angela put down her book without a word and left the room. She appeared a few minutes later with a flustered looking Cathy. 'I'm sorry, Uncle Ethan, I forgot the time.'

Ethan Stopes opened frosted glass doors at the end of the room and Amy caught her breath in surprise. The room in front of her was a modern kitchen diner with a stainless steel range and banks of cupboards and drawers. The work surfaces were black granite and the cabinets glossy white. The floor was covered in a geometric tile pattern, also in black and white. In the dining area a glass-topped table, at least ten feet long, was set for dinner. The chairs were white leather with metal legs and rather

uncomfortable, Amy found, when she later sat on one.

Ethan must have seen the surprise on Amy's face. He gave her a cynical smile. 'My wife redesigned the kitchen before she left me. She's an interior decorator by profession. Celia Cutworth. You may have heard of her.'

Amy was rather pleased she was truthfully able to shake her head. 'No, I'm sorry, but I haven't.' She thought she saw Ethan's mouth curl up in that enigmatic smile of his, but she couldn't be sure.

The room was beautiful in its own way, but completely out of keeping with the rest of the house, and Amy found herself thinking what she would have done given a free hand. The floor would look better covered in warm brown quarry tiles. It probably had been once, before Celia had taken them up to make way for her geometric pattern in black and white. Pale wood, something like sycamore or ash, would lighten the place up just as much as the hard, shiny

white lacquer, and the cooking range should be an Aga, Amy decided, not the stainless steel monstrosity that was daring anyone to try cooking on it. You probably required a degree in mechanics just to turn the thing on.

She realised Ethan Stopes was talking to her and stopped her daydreaming.

'Please help yourself to food.' He waved a hand at a heated hostess trolley standing against the wall. 'Mrs Peacock leaves the food out for us each evening.'

The woman called Angela had already filled her plate and was sitting quietly at the table. Felix helped himself and joined her. Cathy waited for Amy to go in front of her. The food looked delicious. One container held some sort of beef stew, probably a goulash, and there were mashed potatoes and green beans, all piping hot. Standing on the counter beside the trolley was a large glass bowl of trifle.

Amy told herself she needed plenty of food to keep her warm, and filled her plate. Cathy pointed out warm rolls and

a dish of butter, and Felix handed her the white wine she had left in the drawing room and also a glass of red wine.

'Keep the white for dessert,' he said. 'You need a red to go with the beef.'

Amy decided her three weeks here might not be so bad after all.

She smiled her thanks and used the excuse of enjoying her meal to keep quiet and study Angela. The woman fascinated her. She was tall and dark, her hair a thick mane of chocolate curls pulled back into a chignon, and a kind of smouldering beauty. But it was her stillness that made her interesting. And the fact that she couldn't take her eyes off Felix Manning.

The meal was pleasant enough although there seemed an undercurrent of something Amy couldn't quite put her finger on. Cathy sat next to Amy and chatted about nothing in particular. She was nineteen, didn't have a steady boyfriend, and was looking forward to Christmas.

'My mum's coming here for Christmas. My dad died three years ago, so she's on her own now. And uncle Ethan's wife will be bringing the children.' She turned in her chair. 'Why don't you stay, Amy? Christmas is only a few weeks away and it'll be fun.'

Looking at the rather sombre faces around her, Amy rather doubted that. 'I'm only here to help Dr Stopes get his book ready for the publishers, Cathy. He's already finished it, so it's just a matter of helping him sort out chapters and pictures and that sort of thing. I'll only be here for three weeks at the most.' And I want to be in London for Christmas, she thought. With Oxford Street and the bright lights and the decorations. She knew Ethan Stopes had an apartment in London, and she found it hard to understand why he would want to spend Christmas isolated in Norfolk, but that was his choice. Maybe he needed the peace and quiet after working in a busy private hospital most of the time.

She managed to keep awake for coffee in the drawing room, but then made her excuses and found her way up to her bedroom. Someone had put a small electric heater in a corner of the room and a hot water bottle in her bed. Deciding a bath could wait until the morning, she crawled into bed and pulled the soft, fluffy duvet over her. She was asleep in minutes.

2

It took Amy a moment the next morning to work out where she was. She had neglected to pull the curtains over the window, and a dull, grey light seeped reluctantly into the room. She sat up and shivered. Ice patterns on the inside of the window made it impossible to see out. Reaching for her robe she climbed out of bed and breathed on the window, clearing a gap in the ice. Overnight, hoar frost had turned the landscape white. It reminded her of Disneyland. Too beautiful to be real.

But the cold was all too real. She turned on the electric fire, and remembering the big bath, put in the plug and turned on the hot tap, pleased to see scalding water hitting the cold metal. She added just enough cold water to cool the water temperature a little and, leaving the taps running, hopped back

19

into bed. Ten minutes later the bath was three-quarters full. Turning off the taps she added bath oil and slid gratefully into the blissfully warm water. She had no idea what time breakfast was served, but she was pretty sure Ethan Stopes would want to make an early start on his book. By seven thirty, dressed in black jeans and a thick sweater, she was heading downstairs for the kitchen.

Angela was already seated at the table, her book propped up against a pepper mill. She looked up and smiled. 'The men are around somewhere, I expect, and Cathy will be along when she's finished her chores. It's everyone for themselves in the morning. I have juice and cereal, but there's bacon and eggs if you want.'

Amy eyed the range. 'Can you work that thing? It frightens me.'

Angela laughed. 'It frightens me, too, but you don't have to use it. There's a perfectly normal electric hob set into the counter, with an oven underneath.'

Amy found a toaster and popped in two slices of bread. Then she filled a bowl with wheat flakes and poured on milk. Usually she didn't eat much but the cold was making her hungry. Thankfully, the kitchen was nice and warm. Wanting to find out more about Ethan Stopes, Amy pulled up a chair next to Angela.

'Do you mind if I sit with you, or would you rather read?'

'No, please sit down. How long are you staying? I know Ethan has finished his book, so I am not sure what he's asked you to do. You're a professional writer, I believe.'

Amy nodded. 'I've been a journalist for nearly fifteen years, and I've had one full-length novel published, so I know a bit about organising writing, and that's what Dr Stopes wants me to do. Sort out his chapters and where the illustrations should go. That sort of thing.' She hesitated. 'You must have worked for him for a long time. What's he like?'

Angela smiled. 'I've worked for him for five years, and that's not long enough to get to know the man.' She paused, frowning. 'I don't really know what to tell you. He's difficult, opinionated, but also dedicated to his work and determined to make people feel better about themselves. That's what he does, you know. Give people confidence.'

'Even the celebrities who are beautiful already? People with so much money they want to gild the lily?'

'Most celebrities are terrified of failure, Amy, and they have so much more to lose than anyone else.' She looked up. 'Here come the men.'

Ethan walked into the room and looked over at Amy. He nodded approvingly. 'An early starter, I see. Good. 'I need . . . ' he paused, 'I want to get the book finished as quickly as possible.'

Felix took Amy's toast out of the toaster and handed it to her. 'The gooseberry jam is excellent. Mrs Peacock makes it herself.' He sat opposite

Amy and stared into her eyes. 'You have that dewy look that only comes with youth.'

'I'm nearly thirty, Mr Manning,' she said dryly. 'Hardly in the first flush. Could you pass me the butter?'

Angela got to her feet rather abruptly. 'I'll be going. I have work to do.'

Felix let his eyes follow her lazily as she left the room 'I hope it wasn't something I said.'

'Knock it off, Felix,' Ethan said sharply. He looked at Amy. 'I only have coffee in the morning, so when you're ready we'll start on the book.'

Amy looked at him and then at her toast. 'Now?'

Ethan smiled, and the smile completely changed his expression. 'Not right this minute, my coffee is scalding hot still. Finish your breakfast first.'

Fifteen minutes later she followed him eagerly to his study. She was dying to read the book, not just out of idle curiosity, but because she wanted to see if he could write. She had helped with

autobiographies in the past, and some of the so-called celebrities couldn't string two words together. Ethan had only asked for help with the organisation of the book, so he obviously thought he could manage the construction on his own. Amy was prepared to reserve judgement, but she wasn't hopeful.

He sat down behind his desk without offering her a seat. She pulled up a chair and sat opposite him, away from the full heat of the fire burning in the grate. She didn't want to get all sweaty in front of him. He sat looking at a pile of typed pages held together with an elastic band, as if he didn't really know where to start.

'I suppose you need to read it first,' he said at last. He opened a drawer in the desk and reached inside. He took out a brown envelope and tipped an assortment of photos on to the desk. 'These are the photographs. I've put page numbers on them to give you an idea of where I think they should go,

but I'll leave that side of it up to you.'

Amy picked up a print cautiously. She wasn't sure what she was expecting. Before and after photos? Pictures of gory operations, maybe. But she found she was holding a studio portrait of a well-known actress. She held up the photo. 'Are they all like this?'

He smiled, and for a moment she forgot to breathe. Pull yourself together, girl, she told herself. Otherwise you're not going to be able to work with him.

'Not all,' he said, taking the photo from her and looking at it. 'Some are of quite ordinary people with extraordinary problems. I know what you expected, what everyone is going to expect, but this book is supposed to be about my life, not theirs. I have these people's permission to put their photographs in my book, but I have no right to betray their confidence.'

'Your publishers are going to be disappointed. They could even refuse to publish.'

He smiled again, and she felt her

25

pulse quicken. That smile was a killer. 'They've already approved my decision,' he said. 'This is a book about the career of a plastic surgeon, not a kiss-and-tell.'

So he had principles, she thought. Good. She couldn't wait to read the book; more so now she knew there would be no gory photos. Looking at a photo of a celebrity and knowing they'd had cosmetic surgery, but not knowing exactly what had been done, added to the fascination. The reader could study the photo and try to guess.

'OK,' she said. 'I'll shut myself away somewhere for the rest of the day and read your book.' She looked up at him. 'May I take the photos with me?'

'Of course you can.' His eyes twinkled at her. 'Let me know if you work out what work I did on each of them.'

He told her she could stay in the study, but to remember to go for some lunch about mid-day. 'You'll meet Mrs Peacock,' he said with a smile. 'She'll

like you. She loves people who appreciate her food.'

Amy moved into Ethan's chair and
spread the manuscript and photos out
on his desk. He had been exactly right
about where to place the photos, but
she rearranged the chapters as she went
along, ending each one at a point where
you had to carry on reading. The book
was good, probably an automatic
best-seller, but half-way through she
realised she had learned nothing about
the man. Ethan Stopes was still an
enigma.

When Cathy knocked on the door
and came into the room, she was still
engrossed in the book.

'Uncle Ethan said I have to remind
you to eat, and to tell you the book isn't
going anywhere so you can spare an
hour for lunch.'

Amy blinked and stood up. Her eyes
felt gritty and she was stiff from sitting
still. She was glad to get up and follow
Cathy to the kitchen. Mrs Peacock was
a motherly woman with dimples in her

cheeks. She gave Amy a warm smile and asked if she would like an omelette.

'Mushroom or cheese, dear. The mushrooms got picked this morning by my son, Nick. He works for the doctor as well. Handyman and driver. Does most of the gardening, too.' She broke eggs into a bowl and stirred them vigorously with a metal whisk, dropping in a large dollop of cream. 'Not supposed to do that,' she said with a smile, 'but it don't half give you lovely omelettes.'

Amy opted for cheese, being a bit wary of field mushrooms. She looked around the empty kitchen. 'Has everyone else already eaten?'

'Felix and Ethan went out for lunch, and Angela never eats much. Cathy'll be back in a minute. She's just throwing a few more logs on the fires.' Mrs Peacock looked out of the window. 'Looks like snow to me.'

Amy sat down at the table near Mrs Peacock. 'What does Angela do, exactly?'

'She takes care of the doctor's mail

and sorts out the bills and stuff, and she's typed up the book for him on a computer. He dictates into one of those little machines and she types it all out, but I think she must have got stressed with all the extra work. She's not been herself at all, lately.'

'He could use a word-recognition program,' Amy said. 'Or he could learn to type with two fingers, like me.'

Mrs Peacock laughed. 'You heard the one about having a dog?'

'And barking yourself? Yes, I suppose you're right. If he doesn't need to do it, why bother. But all the same, he shouldn't overwork poor Angela.'

Mrs Peacock screwed her cheerful face into a frown. 'He's been a bit peaky himself, come to think of it.' She handed Amy a plate bearing an enormous omelette. 'Working too hard, both of them.'

A few minutes later Cathy came into the room like a tornado. She pulled off a fleece jacket and dropped into a chair next to Amy. 'Too flipping cold out

there to snow. My fingers are dropping off.' She took her omelette and cut it open to look at the mushrooms. 'Wow, these look yummy.'

Amy finished her own food and poured coffee for both of them. 'Is that true? Can it really be too cold to snow? It's always cold in places like Switzerland, and it snows there all the time.'

Cathy shook her head. 'No, Felix said the temperature has to rise a little before it can snow. It probably does that in Switzerland, too. All frozen and icy one minute, and then it warms up a little and down comes the snow.' She smiled. 'It would be fun if it snowed at Christmas, but it never does that here.'

'Be careful what you wish for, young lady,' Mrs Peacock said sternly. 'If it snows too hard your mum won't be able to get here.'

Cathy laughed, and speared a mushroom with her fork. 'A proper white Christmas would still be fun.'

Amy finished her omelette and hurried back to the study. Dr Stopes

was waiting for her. 'Have you finished reading the book?' he asked.

'Almost, and I think it's quite good.' She ignored the look he gave her. 'It has all the right ingredients, but it needs a lot of work. The photo placing is fine, but the chapters need sorting and some of the grammar could be improved.' She laughed at his scowl. 'I'm not trying to suggest you're wrong, but you're not always right. Everyone's writing can be improved upon.'

'Even yours, Miss Franklin?'

'Especially mine, and please call me Amy.'

'Very well.'

She had expected him to suggest she called him Ethan, and when he didn't she found herself strangely disappointed, but if he wanted to keep everything on a formal basis, so be it. He left the room again and she went back to the book, finding mistakes she had missed on the first run through. She was quite looking forward to pointing them out to him.

The next few days passed in a flurry of work. Amy had got into a routine and stopped work at the same time each day. Dr Stopes and Felix Manning had gone back to London, leaving her with Angela and Cathy. The three women worked well together, and Angela got into the habit of popping into the study with two mugs of coffee each morning. Amy was trying to work out what Ethan Stopes was really like, and Angela had known him the longest.

'How long have you worked for him?' Amy asked, as she handed Angela a couple of pages that would have to be retyped. 'Do you always stay here when he goes to London or do you sometimes go with him?'

'I used to go with him, but since he's been writing the book he spends most of his time here at the house. Felix drags him back for a consult now and again, and I think it does Ethan good.'

'Felix is a cosmetic surgeon as well? I thought he was just a friend.'

'Felix is a friend, but he's also a very

good cosmetic surgeon as well. He works at the same hospital as Ethan and they've known one another for years.'

Amy frowned. 'The people who come to Dr Stopes for cosmetic surgery do it out of vanity mostly, don't they? They don't really have anything wrong with them.'

'Ethan thinks they do. He'll tell you the people he operates on really need his help. A tummy tuck after giving birth to several children can completely change a woman's life, and make her feel attractive again.'

If you can afford it, Amy thought darkly. She asked Angela a question that had been puzzling her. 'If Dr Stopes is a surgeon and a consultant, why does he still call himself 'doctor'? I thought he was entitled to call himself 'mister'.'

'He can call himself either,' Angela said. 'But he thought Dr Stopes sounded better as the author of a book on surgery. Mr Stopes doesn't sound very impressive, does it?'

Amy laughed. 'No, you're right. Anyway, I'm not quite sure what to call him. I told him to call me Amy, but he didn't tell me to call him Ethan.'

'Oh, poof,' Angela said. 'The man's playing with you. Call him Ethan like everyone else here. We mustn't let him get above himself and think he can play lord of the manor.'

The next morning Amy looked out of her bedroom window and saw the first few flakes of snow — and Ethan and Felix arrived back at the house.

She had been really good and stuck to cereal and toast each morning since she had arrived, but the sight of the softly falling snow made her feel hungry and she put a frying pan on the hob for bacon and eggs. Staring out of her bedroom window had made her late getting down to breakfast, and she was alone in the kitchen when the outside door flew open and Felix appeared in a flurry of snowflakes.

'Ethan's putting the car away. It's a good job we came back today, otherwise

we might not have made it.'

Amy looked at him worriedly. 'We're not going to get snowed in, are we?'

He pulled off his coat and threw it over a chair. 'Think of weeks snowed in with the two most attractive men in the country. Most women would die for the chance.'

'Do you want bacon?' Amy asked frostily. She wasn't sure what to make of Felix. He gave the impression of being a devil-may-care playboy, but his act didn't quite ring true, and he seemed intent on upsetting Angela as often as he could. Amy was used to watching people, both as a journalist and a novelist, and she studied the play between Felix and Angela with interest. It was a relationship with unusual overtones. If she didn't know better, she would have thought they were in love with one another.

'And eggs,' Felix said in answer to her question, 'and toast and coffee. And if you're cooking you'd better make the same for Ethan. We're both starving.'

Amy looked up as Ethan came into the kitchen. 'Do I cook you both breakfast? Or do the job I'm being paid for and get back to work on your book?' She remembered he had said he only had coffee in the morning.

He looked tired, she thought, as he sat down on one of the hard chairs. And in pain. Her mother had been in a lot of pain once, and Amy had learnt to recognise the signs. She watched as Ethan eased out of his coat and slowly pulled off a pair of fleece-lined gloves. 'Breakfast, please,' he said, taking the coffee Felix had poured for him. He wrapped his hands round the mug and closed his eyes. 'That's better. The train was freezing. I need some food to warm me up.'

Amy was busy with the bacon. She was annoyed at being treated like a cook, but she felt she had probably asked for it. No man is going to say no to having his breakfast cooked for him. She whisked eggs and put butter in a

saucepan while Felix came up beside her and loaded the toaster. As she added the eggs to the saucepan and stirred them, he picked up a slice and turned the bacon. He was very close and she could feel herself getting hot.

He managed to brush against her as he reached for the toast. 'We make a good team, don't we? Scrambled eggs and bacon coming up.' He buttered the toast while she finished off the eggs and then they plated up together. She sat down at the table without a word, and then had to shift her chair as Felix sat so close she couldn't move her arms. She had seen him work this manoeuvre on Angela and she refused to be intimidated. For some reason Ethan looked annoyed.

'You said to cook breakfast first,' she said, but he just waved a hand as if he couldn't care less.

OK, she thought. If you two have fallen out I don't need to know about it. She finished her breakfast, wishing she had stuck to her usual cereal, and

made her way back to the study. An hour later she was busy making pencil marks on the manuscript when Ethan walked into the room.

3

'I need to talk to you about some of the changes I've made,' Amy said, glancing up at him and then back down at the page she was working on. 'I've mucked about with some of the chapters a bit.'

'Mucked about?'

His voice was so chilly she could feel goose bumps break out on her arms. 'You expected me to make changes, didn't you? That was why you hired me.'

He shook his head as if he was clearing it of something nasty and sat down opposite her. 'Of course. Please excuse me. I'm still getting over the journey. Felix always drives rather fast, and in this weather . . .' He took a long breath. 'I feel I should talk to you about my colleague. Felix is . . . that is, he's inclined to be a distraction to women.'

Amy could do frosty as well. 'I assure

you I don't intend to be distracted by Mr Felix Manning, Dr Stopes. And if you would care to read your manuscript when you have the time, I have marked any alterations in pencil for your consideration, and typographical errors in red for Angela to correct on the computer.'

He rubbed his hands together, massaging the knuckles of one hand with the fingers of the other. He saw her watching him and dropped his hands to his lap. 'I am not criticising your work, Amy, and I'll look through the manuscript later today. I'm sure everything is fine.' He got up and walked to the window overlooking the garden. 'It's still snowing.'

She walked over to stand beside him. There was already about an inch of snow on the terrace and the flakes were bigger than when she had last looked. 'I will be able to get home, won't I?'

She had to stand close to him to see out of the small window. He looked down at her. 'I would imagine so. There

is no forecast of heavy snow in the next couple of weeks. Is it important you go home for Christmas? We are having quite a little gathering here and you're welcome to stay.'

Just for a moment she was tempted. But then she remembered how cold it was at night, and having to wait for the bath to fill was still a chore, even though she had found bathing before she went to bed helped her sleep. A quick wash in the morning was an easier option, and enough to freshen her up for the day. I'm adapting, she thought in horror. If I stay here any longer I might find I like living in a freezing old house without any mod cons.

'I have things planned,' she said. 'But thanks for the offer.'

He moved away from her and she missed his warmth. 'Very well. But remember the offer is still open if you change your mind.' He got as far as the door and then turned back. 'It's Saturday tomorrow, and I make a point

of not working anyone over the weekend. Even Mrs Peacock has her two days off. We all muck in and throw some food together, and you'll have to fill your own hot-water bottle, I'm afraid.'

After he left, she finished marking the pages she was working on and considered what she was going to do with her two days off. It wasn't worth going back to London for the weekend, and Ethan obviously expected her to stay at the house. Perhaps she could persuade Angela to go shopping in Norwich, the poor woman looked as if she needed cheering up, and Cathy could come as well if she wanted. A girl's day out would be fun.

By the next morning the snow had stopped and the sun was out. Most of the remaining snow had turned to slush, and Amy decided a trip to Norwich wouldn't pose much of a problem. 'I'll drive if you like,' she offered.

Ethan had the off-roader, but he

liked to keep the car for emergencies, and not, as he put it, for an unnecessary day out shopping. 'What's unnecessary about shopping?' Amy asked him. 'If you can't offer us a spa and sauna when we need it, shopping is the only therapy us girls have left. Besides, you said no more heavy snow showers are expected, so there's no reason for us not to go.'

She was feeling a little stir-crazy after a week at the house and needed to see a real shop again. She had explored the grounds, sat beside the lake, and even walked into the village on one rare occasion, although the few shops in the village street hardly made it worth the effort. Mrs Peacock and Nick walked the two miles every day, but by the time Amy got back she was exhausted and realised how unfit she was. She promised herself more exercise when she got back to London. Maybe she would join a health club.

The drive to the city was really nice. The sky stayed blue and the fields seemed to go on forever. Norfolk might

be flat, but the views were amazing. Amy got Angela to navigate and they took a route through the back lanes until they hit the main road to Norwich. Several times the car splashed through still melting snow, and Amy wondered what the roads would be like if it froze again after dark, but once they had parked in the centre of the city the thought completely left her head. The shops were brilliant. Cathy hadn't been to the city for nearly a year, and wanted to buy the remainder of her Christmas presents. Angela needed a new coat and boots, and Amy found herself looking at handbags and shoes, for which she had a weakness. The designer shops were mostly the same as London, but the prices were lower, and she was sure she would find a bargain.

They ate lunch at a little Italian restaurant and then browsed the big department stores. Amy had hoped they would get most of the return journey over before it got dark, but there was no hope of that. Angela and Cathy wanted

to have tea in one of the little cafes before starting back, so by the time they drove out of the all-day car park it was already dusk.

'There's no sign of freezing at the moment,' Amy remarked optimistically, peering through the windscreen. 'Can you remember the way back, Angela? Norwich was signposted all the way, but I bet Stillworth isn't. We should have borrowed Felix's satnav.'

'We head for Fakenham and then turn off,' Cathy said with confidence. She was sitting in the back examining her purchases. 'I don't remember where we turn off, though,' she added as an afterthought.

'I think I do,' Angela looked worriedly out of the window. 'But it all looks different in the dark.'

Amy didn't answer, she was too busy concentrating on the road. She couldn't see any ice, but every now and again the car slid unnervingly on the slush. 'We've got a way to go yet, but then I want you to look out for the sign to

45

Stillworth,' she told Angela. 'I don't want to miss the turnoff.'

Cathy took out her mobile phone. 'I'll call uncle Ethan,' she said. 'He can give us directions.'

'Not yet,' Amy said hastily. 'I'm sure Angela can remember the way we came.' She was thinking of Ethan's disparaging remarks about shopping. 'If we phone to ask for directions he'll just say 'I told you so'.' She took a breath and eased up on the accelerator as the car slid into a corner. She looked worriedly at the shine on the road's surface. Was that ice, or was the road just wet and slushy with the remainder of the snow? Ten minutes later Angela spotted the turn-off for Stillworth.

Good, Amy thought with satisfaction. Nearly home.

She turned safely on to the side road, but the narrow lane was slick with something that looked suspiciously like ice, and a few moments later the front wheels of the car lost traction com-pletely. She knew what to do in a

rear-wheel skid, but what were you supposed to do when the front wheels were going where they pleased and you had no control over the steering? She remembered a long-ago driving instructor saying 'when in doubt take your feet off everything', so that's what she did. The car moved lazily across the road to nudge a high bank on the left, and then started sliding in the opposite direction. Amy turned the steering wheel frantically, forcing herself not to touch the brake, and eventually the wheels took hold. But by then it was far too late.

'We've gone into a ditch,' Cathy wailed. 'Why didn't you stop?'

'I tried to,' Amy said, turning the ignition off as soon as the car came to a halt. They had finished up sideways in the ditch and she was squashed against the door with Angela practically sitting on top of her. 'Is anyone hurt?'

Angela moved away and gave a little yelp. 'I've done something to my wrist, but otherwise I'm OK. What happened?'

'I think we hit a patch of ice.' Amy tried to open her door but it was stuck against the side of the ditch. 'Can you open your door, Cathy?' she called over her shoulder.

Cathy squirmed up the tilted back seat and managed to open the door. 'I can get out if you want me to, but it's freezing. We may be better off if we stay in the car. At least we won't freeze to death. Can someone phone uncle Ethan, please, and get him to rescue us.'

Angela undid her seatbelt and took her mobile phone out of her pocket with her good hand. She peered at the screen and then started moving the phone around. 'I can't get a signal.'

'Are we going to be stuck here all night?' Cathy sounded near to tears. 'No one will come down this road, I bet. Not until the morning.'

Amy didn't dare turn the ignition back on as she didn't know what damage had been done to the car and, without any heating, hypothermia was a

distinct possibility. 'Try your phone, Cathy, and I'll try mine. They all use different phone masts, I think.'

None of the phones worked, but a few moments later headlights swept across the road and a car turned into the lane. For a moment Amy thought it was going to go past, but then it stopped beside them and a man climbed out of the car, nearly losing his footing on the ice. He peered down into the ditch and Angela pushed open her door. 'We were going to phone home for help, but we can't get a signal,' she said.

'Thank god you're safe. When we came round the corner and saw the car in the ditch we thought you might all be dead.' The man had his wife and two children in his car with him so he didn't want to hang around too long. Amy fished a pen out of her bag and wrote down the number of the phone at the house and the man, whose name was Peter Flanders, promised to call for help as soon as he could get a signal. 'I live a couple of miles from Stillworth

village,' he said. 'So I can call from home, if needs be. No problem.' He stared down at them worriedly. 'Are you sure you're all OK? Do you want me to call the police, or get an ambulance out to you?'

'No thank you,' Amy said quickly. She watched the tail lights of Peter's car disappear with trepidation, and turned in her seat to look at Angela who was nursing her injured hand. 'Your wrist isn't broken, is it? Perhaps we should have called an ambulance after all.'

'Goodness no' Angela gave a little shudder. 'It's not that bad, and can you imagine what the men would say?'

'They're going to say plenty, anyway,' Cathy said gloomily. 'We've crashed Amy's little car and now we're going to freeze to death.'

Twenty minutes later, just as Amy was about to suggest they all cuddled together on the back seat for warmth, a large four-wheel-drive car came hurtling down the lane towards them. Ethan spotted Amy's car at the last

moment and came to a sliding halt, almost joining them in the ditch.

Felix was out of the car and running towards them before Ethan had time to move, and Amy watched in amazement as he almost wrenched off the passenger door and pulled Angela out into his arms.

'What happened? Are you hurt?' Still holding Angela tightly against him, he glared at Amy as she struggled out of the car. 'What were you thinking of, driving all that way in icy conditions? You could all have been killed.'

'It wasn't . . . ' Amy began, trying to pull herself up the icy bank and wishing someone would give her a hand.

Felix didn't give her a chance to finish. 'It wasn't what? We've had freezing temperatures all week, so there was a pretty good chance it would freeze again tonight. You must have realised that.'

Angela pulled herself free of his embrace. 'It wasn't Amy's fault, Felix. She wanted to start back earlier. We

made her stay and have tea.'

Amy felt tears pricking at the back of her eyes. Her ribs were hurting where the seat belt had cut in, both her knees felt bruised, and now Felix was blaming her because her little car had skidded into the ditch. 'All our things are still in the car,' she said, trying to keep her voice steady. 'Shall we get them out or lock them in overnight?'

'Oh, we have to get them out.' Cathy left her uncle and ran towards Amy's car. She looked back at Ethan appealingly. 'Please can we take the presents home, Uncle Felix? They might get stolen if we leave them here all night.'

The three girls were told to get in the back of the Mercedes in the warm, while the men rescued the shopping. Ethan handed Amy her handbag and her car keys. 'I'll arrange for your car to be taken to a garage in the morning. Hopefully, it isn't too badly damaged.' He looked at her soberly. 'Thank goodness no one was badly hurt. It could have been a lot worse.'

The ride back to the house was sub-
dued. Even Cathy kept her usual chatter
to a minimum. Ethan drove slowly and
carefully, the big, four-wheel-drive car
handling the icy patches much better
than Amy's car. When they were almost
home, Felix turned round in his seat
and looked at Amy.

'It wasn't your fault the car went off
the road,' he said. 'I'm sorry I shouted
at you. Ethan skidded on that patch of
ice as well and we nearly joined you in
the ditch. He's driving slowly now, but
you should have seen him on the way
out. He was driving like a maniac.'

Because he was worrying about his
niece, Amy thought, and Felix was
obviously worrying about Angela. She
was just the stupid driver who had
nearly killed them all.

When they got back to the house she
went straight upstairs to soak in a hot
bath. She added a generous amount of
oil and let the sweet smelling water ease
her bruises. Her knee was swollen and
going a funny colour, and there was a

dark mark across her rib cage, but otherwise she seemed to have got off lightly. She had almost dozed off in the warm water when she heard a tentative knock on her bedroom door. She climbed, still dripping, from the bath and grabbed her towelling robe before opening the door. She expected to see Cathy, and was shocked to see Ethan standing before her.

Smiling his usual enigmatic smile, he handed her a glass of amber liquid. 'Brandy to warm you up.' His look was appreciative. 'Although you look positively glowing at the moment.'

His smile confused her and she backed away, clutching the robe tightly around her. He followed her into the bedroom, still holding the glass. 'I intend to make sure you drink this, you've had a nasty shock today.'

The only real shock, she thought, was having Ethan Stopes in her bedroom. She took the glass he handed her and took a sip, almost choking as the strong spirit hit the back of her throat. 'Wow,'

she said. 'It's ages since I had a brandy.'

He suddenly realised that she was dripping on to the wooden floor and backed towards the door. 'I'm sorry if I got you out of your bath. Finish your drink and come downstairs when you're ready. We've got a good fire going.' He hesitated in the doorway. 'I'm glad you weren't hurt, Amy. I've grown fond of you since you've been here, and I wouldn't want anything to happen to you.'

As the door shut behind him, she plopped down onto the bed, not caring if she made a wet patch. Fond was not the word she had expected to hear and, if she was honest, not really the word she had wanted to hear, but it would have to do for now.

The rest of the brandy went down much more smoothly, and standing in front of the mirror wrapped in a towel a few moments later, she realised how she must have looked to Ethan Stopes. She had removed all her makeup before she got in the bath, and her hair was

hanging in wet rat's tails round her ears. The robe she had brought with her was an old one, pinched from a hotel room many years before, and the nail varnish on her toes needed touching up. No man in his right mind gets a woman out of a bath and gives her a brandy. Not without some sort of warning first.

She took her time dressing and drying her hair. She knew no one dressed up for dinner, but she felt the occasion called for more than a jumper and jeans, so she chose a long-sleeved dress in pale lavender jersey and draped a matching cardigan round her shoulders for warmth. She'd warmed her pale face with a touch of blusher and chosen dark tights to hide the bruises on her knees. Luckily no one could see the dark line across her ribs.

When Amy walked into the drawing room she saw a table by the fire holding a bottle of champagne and glasses. The men had excelled themselves in the kitchen and dinner was almost ready.

Angela had also dressed up for the evening. She wore a sheath of red wool with a shiny black belt, and she looked, Amy thought, absolutely stunning. Felix couldn't take his eyes off her. Poor little Cathy just looked cold. She was standing by the fire cuddled in a thick cream sweater and jeans, a glass of wine already in her hand.

Smiling, Felix handed Amy a tulip glass of champagne. 'Am I forgiven?'

She smiled back. 'I should be asking that question. We were very foolish to stay so late in the city.' She held up her glass. 'Here's to still being alive.'

Ethan walked over and gave her one of his dark and moody looks. 'It's snowing now on top of the ice. No one will be going anywhere tomorrow.'

'Does that mean my car won't get moved?' she asked anxiously. 'It won't do it any good to stay in that ditch.'

'Driving into the ditch in the first place didn't do it much good, either,' Ethan said pointedly. 'I'll get it pulled out tomorrow if I can, but the garage

won't want to come out on a Sunday.'

His moods changed so quickly, Amy was never sure what to expect. He went from being absolutely charming, to someone who seemed to have an enormous chip on his shoulder. What he had to be so angry about, she had no idea.

Felix provided her with a couple of aspirin for the pain in her knees. 'Taken with champagne, they work much better.' His smile was followed by a frown. 'Angela has sprained her wrist quite badly, I think.' He looked across the room to where Angela was holding a drink in her left hand. 'I don't think it's broken, but she's not going to be able to type on the computer for a few days.'

'How about Ethan's book?' Amy asked. 'I need to get the alterations finished before I leave, and the finished manuscript has to be at the publishers before Christmas Eve.'

Felix shook his head. 'Until a doctor has taken a look, I don't know how bad

it is, but she'll have to rest her hand for a while. I suggested a sling, but she won't hear of it. Can you type alterations straight on to the computer?'

'I suppose so, but Ethan needs to check everything first, and that takes time. I make my alterations, and normally Angela would type them up and print out a copy for Ethan, who then alters everything and gives the manuscript back to Angela to type up again. It all takes time, Felix, time we don't have.'

'Then he'll have to sit with you and you'll both have to work directly on to the computer. Angela can't use a keyboard. I won't let her.'

She looked across the room at Ethan as he refilled his glass with champagne. 'He won't like it.'

'He doesn't have to like it, but if he wants this book out on time he's going to have to do it. He hasn't got any choice. He needs to get the book finished.' Felix put a finger under Amy's chin to tilt her head up and kissed her lightly on the

lips. 'Thanks Amy.'

She put a hand to her lips, feeling herself flush, and glanced over at Ethan. He was looking back at her, his expression unreadable.

'Damn,' she whispered softly to herself.

4

By morning the world outside was white and Amy shivered as she crawled out of bed. The window gave her a view of fairyland. Large flakes of soft snow were falling and a layer of snow, like a white duvet cover, had already smoothed out the sharp corners of the landscape. She was worried about her car. It was her only link with the outside world, and now both circumstance and nature seemed to be combining to keep her at the house.

She turned on the electric heater, and climbed back into bed. A knock on the door had her reaching for her robe and, this time, her hairbrush. Cathy, clad in a pink fluffy dressing gown and slippers to match, bounded into the room like an excited puppy.

'Have you seen outside? Isn't it great? We might have a white Christmas.'

Amy jumped out of bed again and ran to the window. 'It's over two weeks to Christmas. The snow can't possibly last that long, can it? Besides, I have to get my car out of the ditch.' She let the curtains drop back over the window. 'I'm due to go home on Friday.'

Cathy flopped down on Amy's bed. 'Oh, stop being such a party-pooper. I didn't mean it would snow for two whole weeks. I'm sure you'll be able to go home if you want. You can always get a train.'

Feeling really mean, Amy sat down next to Cathy. 'I'm sorry. A white Christmas would be really wonderful, especially here. I can just imagine log fires and carols round the tree. Do you have a tree?'

Cathy nodded. 'Ethan gets a really big one that goes right up to the ceiling in the hall. We all decorate it on Christmas Eve. Ethan's children love it.'

'How old are they?'

'Molly is six and George is almost

ten, I think. George goes to boarding school because Celia has to be away a lot, but Molly spends most of her time with a nanny, or with me and my mum. She's like my little sister. Celia has a flat in London and a place somewhere in Spain for the holidays, but last year she sent the children to a summer camp in America. My mum offered to have them both, and Ethan wanted them to stay here with him, but Celia made them go. Molly didn't like it.'

Which said it all, Amy thought. 'How long have they been divorced, Celia and Ethan?'

Cathy rolled over on the bed to look at Amy. 'Why?'

Amy wished she didn't go red quite so easily. It was a juvenile trait in a grown woman. 'No particular reason.'

Cathy laughed. 'Mum says curiosity killed the cat. They've been properly divorced three years. Celia went back to using her old name and got this posh job. She started to go away on business all the time and Ethan tried to g

custody of the children, but the judge said they should be with their mother.' She sighed. 'Only they never are.'

'Never mind,' Amy said brightly. 'They'll all be together at Christmas.'

'Yeah,' Cathy said gloomily. 'That's the only thing that might spoil a really good holiday.' She wriggled off the bed. 'You need to get dressed. I'll see you at breakfast.'

So Ethan had tried to get custody of his children. That was interesting. Amy washed quickly, considering the implications. What had he intended to do with the children while he was working in London, she wondered? Farm them out, probably, the same as their mother, which was why the judge had given her custody. Just for a moment, Amy wished she could stay. Christmas at the house promised to be really interesting.

Sunday breakfast was a much more relaxed affair that the rather rushed meals during the week. Angela put a big pan of bacon in the oven to keep warm and Cathy whisked eggs that could be

either scrambled or made into an omelette. The men were not idle, either. Felix was busy with the toaster and Ethan had the coffee grinder going. Amy took over the omelette making. There were no mushrooms, but she found ham and cheese in the fridge, and cooking, she decided, was quite therapeutic first thing in the morning.

After breakfast, Cathy suggested a snowball fight, but Amy and Angela declined. 'We got cold enough yesterday,' she said. 'I want to keep warm today.'

Ethan rubbed his hands in front of the fire, flexing his long, surgeon's fingers. 'I think I'll opt out this time, too. I want to go through the manuscript again.'

'No work on a Sunday, remember?' Felix said lightly. 'Your rule, old boy.'

'I need to get this done, Felix.' Ethan's face was tight with annoyance. 'Angela can't use the keyboard, and Amy has to go home at the end of the week. We're on a very tight schedule

now. Perhaps you should remember that.'

Amy expected Felix to come back with a sarcastic retort, but he looked at Ethan worriedly. 'Are you all right'

Amy watched Ethan take a breath, fighting to get his temper under control. 'Of course. Sorry. Just a headache. I'll take another couple of pills and I'll be fine.' He walked out of the room and a few seconds later, Felix followed him.

Angela walked across the room. 'What was that all about?'

Amy shook her head. 'I'm not sure. Ethan wanted to read through his manuscript again, and Felix reminded him nobody is supposed to work on Sunday. Then Ethan had a little temper tantrum.'

Angela looked puzzled. 'That's not like him — but he hasn't been himself lately. He's usually so easygoing he lets people walk all over him. Anything for a quiet life. But lately he's been really irritable.' She shrugged. 'Something to

do with the book, maybe. He's probably got a heavy schedule at the hospital in the New Year, so he promised to get the book to the publishers before Christmas.' she held up her hand, her wrist strapped in an elastic bandage, 'And now he's never going to make it on time.'

'He might. I'm going to see if I can get him to work directly on to the computer with me' She smiled at Angela. 'Cut out the middle man, who seems to be injured.'

Angela looked crestfallen. 'I feel really bad about all this. Your car's in a ditch, I can't work, and Ethan's going to miss his deadline. We shouldn't have gone to Norwich, should we?'

'No point in agonising about it now, the damage is done.' She walked to the window. 'Look, Felix and Cathy are building a snowman.'

Angela peered out into the garden. 'He's like a little kid, sometimes. No, I take that back. Felix is like a little kid most of the time.'

Amy was used to working on her own, and she knew being close to Ethan for any length of time was going to be difficult. For some reason the man made her act like an idiot. She found herself watching the way his mouth moved when he spoke, and the habit he had of raising one eyebrow, like a question mark, when she had confused him in some way. The way they had been working, with Angela as a go-between, had worked fine, but the two of them in front of one computer screen might get a little too cosy.

She spent a lovely morning in front of the fire reading, but after a big lunch of burgers and baked beans put together by Cathy, she felt she might have been too self-indulgent. Her bruised knee had become stiff, her back was aching, and she needed to work off the calories. Clad in boots, a quilted jacket, and a thick scarf and gloves, she set off for a walk through the gardens towards the lake. The sky was thick and grey, with the promise of more snow to

come, but the landscape was stunning. She missed the ducks, who were probably warm and dry somewhere, but then a lone mallard appeared and gave a little skating exhibition on the ice. She laughed out loud as the bird lost its footing and slid to the edge of the pond on its rear end.

Feeling much better, she started back towards the house only to stop in her tracks when she heard voices coming from the terrace.

'I don't want to talk about it, Felix. You made yourself perfectly clear last time, so there's no point in going over it again.'

'I don't understand why things had to change. We were fine as we were.'

'No we weren't.' Angela's voice was soft now. 'We'd been seeing one another for three years, Felix, and I didn't know you thought it was an open relationship. I thought we had more than that.'

Amy wanted to move. She didn't want to eavesdrop on what was obviously a very private conversation,

but she couldn't get back into the house without being seen. Just as she was about to make a noisy approach to the terrace, so they'd hear her coming, Felix spoke again.

'I was just flirting, Angela. Give me a break. If it matters that much, I won't do it again.'

'Can you be absolutely, one hundred percent, certain of that? I need commitment, Felix. I want to get married and have kids before its too late, and you don't. It's as simple as that. I'm going back to Italy after Christmas to see my parents, and I may decide to stay.'

Amy crashed about a bit in the underbrush before making her appearance on the terrace. Felix had gone but Angela was standing waiting for her.

'How much did you hear?'

'Not a lot. The last few sentences.' She pulled off her gloves and rubbed her hands together. 'It's scary when you realise your biological clock won't carry on ticking forever. I don't know

anything about kids, and I've never really wanted any, but I don't want the option taken away from me. I still want to be able to choose what I do with my life.'

'And so does Felix,' Angela said. 'That's our problem.'

The two women walked into the house together, and Amy sat down to pull off her boots while Angela headed upstairs.

Ethan called to Amy from the study. 'Can I see you in here for a minute?'

She slipped out of her damp jacket. 'May I change first?'

'I'll only keep you for a few moments,' he said impatiently. 'I need to talk to you about my book.'

She refrained from reminding him it was Sunday. Probably not a good idea. He sounded tetchy again, and she guessed Felix had mentioned the proposed working arrangements. Did she really want to be sitting next to this angry man for hours on end? She hung her coat on the back of a chair near the

fire and laid her gloves and scarf on the rug in front of the glowing embers, deliberately keeping Ethan waiting. It was about time he realised he couldn't snap his fingers and expect her to come running.

She walked into the study with as much dignity as she could muster in her socks, and stood before him like a schoolgirl in front of the headmaster. She knew it would annoy him, and it did.

'Sit down, for goodness sake. You look as if you're expecting a caning.'

She sat without answering, although she could think of quite a few good retorts, and he looked up and saw the smile on her face.

His frown disappeared and he smiled back at her. 'Forget I said that, will you? Even though I won't be able to. I shall probably take the thought to bed with me.' This time he laughed out loud. 'I think I had better stop now, before I fall into that big hole I'm digging myself.'

Amy realised it was the first time she

had heard him laugh, and what an amazing difference it made. The little lines at the sides of his eyes really were laughter lines. She wondered what had changed him from a happy man into a miserable one, and then she looked down at his hands where they rested on the desk. She had seen that kind of redness and swelling before, and she knew the pain that went with the illness. Her mother crying was the thing she remembered most about her childhood.

Ethan was a surgeon. His very soul rested in his hands.

He saw her looking and thrust his hands under the desk, but not quickly enough. 'It's just the cold.'

'No, it isn't. It's rheumatoid arthritis. My mother had it.' She took one of his hands and held it, and he didn't try to stop her. She looked at his fingers, his beautiful surgeon's fingers, and it filled her with dread. 'How bad?'

'Bad enough to stop me operating. I've given in my notice at the hospital.

That's why I'm writing the book. I have to pay for this house and my flat in London, and the children's education. Besides which, Celia has two houses, and expects to be kept in the style to which I have let her become accustomed.'

'Insurance?'

'Medical insurance to cover my treatment. But not sufficient to keep two children at boarding school and an expensive ex-wife.' He closed his eyes. 'I agreed to a deadline for the book, and if I don't meet it I'll have to start looking for another publisher.'

'It's my fault,' Amy said. 'I crashed the car and that's why Angela sprained her wrist.' She moved round the desk so she could look into his eyes. 'I'm so sorry, Ethan.'

'Please don't feel sorry for me.' The ice was back in his voice and she wanted to slap him.

'I wasn't feeling the least bit sorry for you. I was just saying I was sorry I injured Angela, and you're so bad

tempered no one is ever likely to feel sorry for you, so I wouldn't worry about it if I were you.'

'But you're not me, are you?' He scowled at her. 'Felix is the only person who knows about this, I haven't even told Celia, so I would appreciate it if you didn't tell anyone.'

'Sure you wouldn't like me to put it on Face Book?' She wanted to hear him laugh again but she was right out of jokes. 'This is silly,' she said at last. 'We both want to get the book out on time, so why are we wasting time arguing? The pain is usually controllable, Ethan, so take another couple of pills or whatever medication you're on, and stop being a martyr. My mother used to do that, and it didn't help anyone, least of all her.'

'I just took two but they take a while to work.' He had the grace to look shamefaced. 'Most of the time my hands are fine, but I can't trust them any more. I'm sorry, Amy. I know you just want to help.'

'Well then, shut up and let me. I worked out a plan with Angela so we can get the manuscript to the publishers before the deadline. Instead of messing around with the hard copy, we work directly on to the computer. We'll go through each page together and get a finished copy out in a few days.' She knew she was being optimistic because she could only stay until the end of the week. That was her deadline.

'It's nearly finished, isn't it?'

She saw the hope in his eyes and wished with all her heart she could say yes, but she knew Ethan would only settle for perfection and that is what she intended to give him. 'We still have some work to do. I've shuffled the chapters around to give the book more impact and you need to OK everything I've done. But the worst is over. All the pictures are where you want them, although I've done away with some of your celebrities.' She smiled at him. 'Not literally, of course.'

He stood up and came round to her

side of the desk. 'I never imagined I would become a bitter and twisted old man, but it seems I'm well on the road. I'm sorry about your mother.'

'That's all right. You can feel sorry for other people, just don't feel sorry for yourself. The illness can be painful and debilitating, but it's not life threatening.'

He raised his question mark eyebrow. 'What happened to your mother then? How did she die?'

Amy laughed. 'She isn't dead. My mother and father live in Florida. The climate seems to suit her better than damp, cold old England, and she's really well at the moment. I'm going out to see them both in the New Year.'

He smiled at her. 'Thank you, Amy, for bringing sunshine into my life on a grey December day.'

She got to her feet and stood looking at him. The urge to kiss him was almost irresistible, and he seemed to feel the same current of warmth between them. As if reading her mind, he bent down

and kissed her lightly on the lips. 'Felix isn't the only one who can say thank you with a kiss.'

Except this was different. His lips lingered on hers for a moment and the surge of electricity was mind blowing. She staggered, catching hold of the back of the chair for support, wanting to throw herself into his arms and beg for more. But by the time her head cleared he was shuffling papers on his desk, waiting for her to leave.

She went down to the kitchen early to find Angela in an apron trying to stuff a chicken. 'Thank goodness they've been drawn and quartered, or whatever it is they do to chickens. I couldn't cope with one that actually looked like a bird.'

Amy studied the two trussed chickens on the work surface. 'You're right. I can't imagine either of these running round the yard pecking up corn.' She washed her hands in the sink and set to work on the other chicken.

'Not any more, anyway.' Felix stood

watching them from the doorway. 'For some reason Ethan is full of the joys of spring and asked me to open another bottle of champagne. Stick those two creatures in the oven, and come and join me for a drink.'

'Shan't be a tick.' As he walked out of the kitchen, Angela opened a bag of frozen roast potatoes and tipped them into a baking dish. 'Can you have parsnips with chicken?' Without waiting for an answer, she opened another bag. 'No doubt we'll find out soon enough.'

When Amy walked into the drawing room, Cathy already had a glass of champagne in her hand. Felix held up both hands in surrender before Amy could have a go at him. 'Don't worry, I've limited her to one.' His eyes lit up at the sight of Angela and Amy thought how stupid love was. Compromise was all that was needed, but neither of them would give an inch. She wished they'd sort out their problems and get on with their lives. Hopefully, together.

Her own heart flipped as Ethan

appeared and Amy knew she was blushing. She turned away quickly, but he came over and rested a hand lightly on her shoulder. 'You look very nice tonight.' For a moment she couldn't remember what she was wearing. Suddenly stripped of all coherent thought, her mind was a blank. 'Your car has been taken to the garage in the village,' he went on, 'and an initial check suggests the damage may not be too severe. I've asked them to make sure the car is roadworthy by the end of the week.'

'Thank you.' Her voice came out as a croak and she cleared her throat, hurrying towards the kitchen. 'I'll check on the chickens.' Opening the door to a hot oven would give her an excuse for a pink face. She needed to get home, she thought, as she prodded the chickens and turned the potatoes. She had only known Ethan a couple of weeks, and he was crotchety and bad tempered most of the time, but she couldn't get him out of her thoughts. Her heart skipped

a beat when he came into the room, and she missed him when he was gone. But he was at least ten years older than she was, and he had enough baggage to fill a bus. It was definitely time she left.

5

The first few days working with Ethan were fine. He listened to what she had to say, and seemed to accept that she was the expert and being paid to do a job. She tried to put out of her mind the fact that he was only a few inches away most of the time. When he leant over to watch something she was doing on the screen, she could feel his breath on her cheek. And sometimes he stood behind her, his hands resting lightly on her shoulders, while he made suggestions and she transferred them to the computer screen.

On her suggestion, because warmth seemed to help with the pain in his hands, he wore soft fleece gloves most of the time he was with her, and once, because he was so impatient, he tried to type something on the keyboard with his gloved fingers. Amy had been

unable to stop herself laughing, and after a minute he had joined in.

It was the laughter that did it, she told herself later. Otherwise he would never have kissed her. This kiss was nothing like the kiss that had gone before. This kiss was deep and wonderful and she wanted it to go on forever, but in the end it was she who broke away first, and she still had no idea why she did that.

Who's afraid of commitment now, she asked herself bitterly, as he turned away from her. 'Ethan?' she said tentatively, but he shook his head.

'We're both tired and overworked, Amy, and I had no right to take advantage of you. Please forgive me. The painkillers sometimes affect my judgement.'

What did that mean? At least he didn't ask her to do the impossible and forget it ever happened. She wanted to throw herself into his arms and beg him to kiss her again, but the moment had passed, and he hardly spoke to her for

83

the rest of the day.

On Wednesday, two days before Amy was due to pick up her car and go home, everything came to a head.

Celia Cutworth arrived with the children.

Amy was having her usual afternoon tea with Angela when the study door burst open and Celia stood in the doorway. She stared at the two women as if she had suddenly come upon an alien life form.

'Where's Ethan?'

Angela blinked but didn't move. 'I have no idea.'

'Well, I would have thought he'd be around to welcome his children. We've come a long way to be ignored.'

Amy kept quiet as Angela got to her feet. 'We weren't expecting you until Friday, Celia. Ethan is around some-where. I'm sure he hasn't left the country. Would you like a cup of tea?'

'I don't drink tea, but coffee would be nice.' Looking somewhat mollified, Celia sank down on to the scuffed sofa

and took off her suede boots. She was wearing a long sweater in soft black wool and black leggings, her designer-cut blond hair falling loose to her shoulders. 'We came today because the weather forecast is predicting more snow and the children would have been devastated if we couldn't get here. We came by train and took a taxi from the station. I knew Ethan would be working on his damned book, and complain if we asked him to pick us up.'

'Felix would have picked you up from the station.'

Celia shuddered. 'The man's a lunatic, and he drives like one too, so no thanks.' She looked at Amy. 'Are you the ghost writer? I knew he'd never get the book done on his own. I suppose he's going to get you to write it, and then say he did it himself. What a hypocrite.'

'That's not it at all,' Amy said, rushing to Ethan's defence. 'He finished the book before I got here. I'm

just helping him edit. It's an amazing piece of work.'

'My, my,' Celia gave Amy an appraising look. 'So he can still pull the young ones, can he? You surprise me. I would have thought he was past it.'

Angela jumped in before Amy could get out the sharp retort on the tip of her tongue. 'Where are the children, Celia? You haven't just left them to run around, have you?'

'Oh, stop fussing, Angela. Cathy is looking after them.' She pulled a silver cigarette case out of her bag and took out a cigarette. 'I know Ethan doesn't like it, he thinks I'm going to poison the children or something, so just don't tell him.' She lit the cigarette and drew in smoke, exhaling in Amy's face. 'So how long are you staying, ghost writer?'

'Until the book's finished,' Amy answered sweetly. It took more than a bitchy ex-wife to intimidate her. She waved a hand in front of her to clear the smoke. 'Sorry, but I'd hate to get secondary lung cancer.'

'Yes, I agree with that.' Angela said. 'Could you put the cigarette out, please, Celia. We all have to work in here.'

Obviously annoyed, Celia threw her cigarette on the fire and looked pointedly at Angela. 'You did offer me a cup of coffee, if you remember.'

'Of course. I'm just on my way to the kitchen. There's plenty in the pot so you can help yourself.'

Celia zipped up her boots and followed Angela out of the room, but just before she reached the door she turned round and looked at Amy. 'Christmas here is always a family affair, but I'm sure you'll be gone by then, won't you?'

Amy debated raiding the wine cabinet. She was feeling so wound up she thought she might burst at any moment. How could Ethan have stayed married to that woman for so long? She only needed a pointy hat to be right in character.

Ethan had driven Mrs Peacock into

the village to pick up the Christmas groceries and Amy knew he wouldn't be back for at least another half hour, so she decided to go in search of the children. She wanted to find out which parent they took after, and they weren't hard to find. The sound of laughter drew her to Cathy's bedroom. She knocked, and then let herself in. A pillow fight was in progress and no one had heard her knock on the door.

Three faces looked at her guiltily, and she knew she would have recognised the children anywhere. The boy was like a miniature version of his father, while the little girl, sitting on Cathy's bed in a mess of tangled bedclothes, was a clone of her mother. White blond curls framed a cute, heart-shaped face, while big blue eyes regarded Amy curiously.

'You're new. Who are you?'

'I'm Amy.' She looked at Cathy. 'Aren't you going to introduce me?'

Cathy grinned. 'Formal introductions coming up. Amy, this is George Matthew and Molly Catherine, the

children of Dr Ethan Stopes, the famous cosmetic surgeon.'

'We used to be Stopes,' George said. 'But now we're Cutworths, 'cos that's mum's name, and dad left us.'

'I didn't know that,' Amy said slowly. 'I thought your mother took you away.'

George shook his head stubbornly. 'We all lived in the house in London, but then dad bought this house and came to live here without us.'

Cathy's eyes met Amy's over the children's heads. 'Because Celia got the London house in the divorce settlement,' she said quietly, 'and Ethan had to move out. He bought this place originally as a bolthole, a retreat from his work, but now he lives here most of the time.'

'But you come to stay here quite often, don't you.' Amy said, trying to get the conversation back on solid ground.

'At Christmas,' Molly piped up, not to be outdone by her brother. 'We come here at Christmas and Daddy digs up a

tree. On Christmas Day we get presents under the tree.'

Amy nodded, smiling. 'Father Christmas brings the presents and puts them under the tree, doesn't he?'

Molly looked puzzled. 'Daddy puts our presents under the tree, so does Mummy. Father Christmas is a story.' She looked at her brother for confirmation. 'You said he's a story, didn't you, George? Like on television.'

George laughed self-consciously. 'No point in teaching her lies.'

'No, of course not.' Amy backed towards the door. Was he really only nine years old? 'I'm spoiling your fun,' she said, 'so I think I'd better go.' She looked at Cathy apologetically and waved a hand at the children. 'I'll see you all at dinner.'

She went back to the study and sat staring at the fire. Perhaps George really was too old to believe in Father Christmas, but Molly was only six. She sighed and went back to her desk. What did she know about children?

She worked for another hour, hoping to get Celia Cutworth and the children out of her head, but then she came to a point where she needed Ethan beside her to agree to her alterations. She looked at her watch. He must have got back from the village by now, so he'd probably got sidetracked on the way to the study, and she could guess who was responsible. The last thing he needed right now was an ex-wife adding to his problems.

She wished she could stand under a hot shower, but a quick splash in four inches of water had to do. She stood in front of her wardrobe staring at the few items inside. The trouble was, most of her clothes were still at her flat in London. Normally, she wouldn't agonise quite so much about what to wear, but today was different. Nothing too fancy, she thought, she didn't want to look as if she was in competition with Celia, but something other than her usual jeans. She eventually decided on her black skirt, because the red top she

had bought in Norwich looked wonderful with it. Sheer tights and flat black pumps completed the outfit, and she smiled at her reflection. Maybe she was competing after all.

She went downstairs early because the last thing she wanted to do was make an entrance. She hated that moment when you walk into a room and everyone stops talking. At first she thought the room was empty, but then she saw Ethan standing by the window. He turned to look at her.

'Thank goodness it's you. I thought it might be Celia, and I'm hoping she takes so long changing we can go straight in to dinner without having to bother with polite conversation. Mrs Peacock offered to put the children to bed. I hate asking Cathy all the time. She's only a child herself.'

'Don't let her hear you say that,' Amy said with a smile. She walked over to stand by Ethan. The blinds hadn't been drawn and she looked out at the dark garden. Spot lights gleamed amongst

the flower borders. 'Is that snow?'

'Yes. It started again about an hour ago.' He looked at her seriously. 'I hate having to say this, Amy, but I think you should go home. If you pack your things tonight, Felix can run you to the village tomorrow. I've just spoken to the garage and your car is ready.'

Amy felt cold, as if someone had plunged her into freezing water. Surely one kiss couldn't have brought this on? 'Why?' she asked fearfully. 'Is it my work? Or did Celia tell you to get rid of me? I didn't mean to upset her.'

He was silent for so long she thought she was going to faint. How could he send her away? He needed her. The book wasn't finished and he couldn't finish it without her.

'Amy, my dear,' he said at last. 'Your work is beyond reproach, and if you upset my ex-wife, I can only applaud you; but it's snowing, and if you don't leave tomorrow you may be marooned here over Christmas.'

She laughed with relief and stood on

tiptoe to kiss him lightly on the cheek. 'I thought you were fed up with me and wanted to get rid of me. I'll stay as long as you need me.'

'Well, well, well,' Felix said from the doorway. 'You are a dark horse, Ethan, old man. Would you like me to leave you two alone?'

Ethan smiled at his friend. 'Amy's agreed to stay in spite of the weather. We'll just have to keep our fingers crossed we can still get her home in time for Christmas. I wouldn't want her to get stranded here.'

'Is that so?' Felix drawled. 'You could have fooled me.'

If Amy hadn't been watching him so closely, she wouldn't have noticed, but just for a moment Ethan looked flustered. 'Of course, we'd all like Amy to stay, but she has commitments elsewhere.' He changed the subject. 'Have you seen Celia, Felix? She's disappeared somewhere. She just dumps the children on whoever will take them. Cathy has been playing with them, and now

Mrs Peacock is putting them to bed. I can't understand why the authorities gave her custody.'

'We've spoken about that, haven't we, Ethan. Celia said you worked all hours of the day and night, and wouldn't have time to give two children the care and attention they deserve, and the court believed her. But now things have changed, haven't they?'

Ethan ran a hand through his hair. 'But she didn't want them. As far as she's concerned they're just a nuisance. She sent George to boarding school, and a nanny has Molly most of the time, so why did she ask for custody?'

'So you wouldn't get it,' Felix stated flatly. 'She got the London apartment, and she'd have this house as well, if she could get her hands on it. Not because she wants it, but because it's yours. She won't let you have the children because she knows you want them.'

Of course, Amy thought, if Ethan gave up operating and took a consultancy position instead, he could fit his

hours round the children. That was what Felix had meant about things changing.

Ethan sighed. 'The publishers are promoting me as an acting cosmetic surgeon and I signed a two book deal. They can't find out I'm giving up surgery, not until the first book is on the shelves, at any rate, then I can say I just found out I have arthritis and have to give up operating.'

'What about your own doctor?' Amy asked. 'I know about patient confidentiality, and all that, but he'll know you lied.'

Felix and Ethan looked at one another, and Amy sighed. 'You haven't seen a doctor, have you?'

Ethan smiled. 'I know what's wrong with me, Amy. I do have some medical training, remember, and I can get hold of all the drugs I need. I'm on normal painkillers at the moment and they work fine.'

Most of the time, Amy thought darkly, but not all the time.

Celia swept in swathed in black jersey and expensive perfume. She looked fantastic. Amy considered giving up there and then, but she put on a brave face. After all, it was all about money really, and whether you had it or not. The highlights in Celia's hair would have cost Amy several months' wages, and she doubted they sold the perfume Celia was wearing on eBay. But finding bargains could be fun, she told herself philosophically. The slinky black dress had been designed to hug every curve, and Celia did seem to have more curves and fewer wrinkles than most women her age. Being married to a cosmetic surgeon obviously had its advantages.

Mrs Peacock had put Molly to bed, but George had been allowed to stay up. He had been dressed, no doubt by his mother, in long trousers and a white shirt that would have looked better on a little old man. Amy wished she had stuck with her jeans just to make a point. No one should be forced to wear uncomfortable clothes, although the

stiletto-heeled shoes Celia wore were certainly not designed for comfort — or even for walking, come to that — and someone should have explained to the woman what spike heels did to a real wood floor.

Celia made straight for Ethan and planted a kiss on his cheek. Ethan looked surprised and Amy smiled to herself, remembering her earlier kiss in almost the same place. Which one would he remember, she wondered.

Needing a drink, she walked to the sideboard and poured herself a glass of white wine. This was a chardonnay and she sniffed it appreciatively. Apple and citrus, with a hint of melon. The wine slid down as easily as she had expected and she picked up the bottle to inspect the label, but when she looked across the room she caught Celia looking at her with a knowing smile. Amy sighed. Now she had a reputation as an alcoholic. She realised she was going to have to watch how much she drank at dinner

if she wanted to keep her wits about her.

Angela arrived with Cathy and Amy noticed they had both dressed up more than usual.

Mrs Peacock called them to eat and Celia regarded her kitchen with pride. 'It's taken a bit of a bashing, darling,' she said to Ethan. 'You have to treat top-of-the range units like this with a bit of respect.'

'Believe it or not,' Ethan said dryly, 'we actually cook things in here. A working kitchen is not going to look like a showroom model.'

Celia ran her hand over the shiny stainless steel of the range. 'This has worn well.'

'Because none of us use it,' Angela said. 'This may be a working kitchen, but that is not a working cooker. It's too big. One jacket potato in that oven would use enough electricity to heat Buckingham Palace.'

'Well, you should have gas laid on, like normal people. I don't know how

you live in this place Ethan.' She looked around with a frown. 'But I suppose I can do something with it before you sell it.'

'I beg your pardon?' Ethan's voice held more ice than the landscape outside the window.

Celia smiled. 'I need an increase in my allowance, darling. The interior decorating business has gone downhill a bit since the recession.' She slipped into a chair at the table and spread a napkin on her lap. 'If you sell this mausoleum of a place you can easily afford to give me more money.'

Her words hung in the air while everyone, including George, stared at Ethan.

He took his time settling himself at the head of the table. 'I have enough money to manage on at the moment, thank you, Celia. I'm sorry you're finding it hard to adjust to the recession, but the children's school fees are taken care of, and you're getting quite enough out of me already, so

there is absolutely no reason for me to sell this house.'

Celia kept her eyes fixed on Ethan's face. She looked, Amy thought, like a snake readying itself to strike.

'But I think there is.' Celia took a slow sip of her wine. 'Rumour has it you haven't been operating much lately. I've heard of surgeons who lose their nerve as they get older. And what about the book, Ethan? The book you've been working so hard on? I know the publishers set a deadline, and it's not going to be finished on time, is it? Not now Angela's hurt her hand and can't do your typing for you.'

'Yes, it is, actually,' Amy said matter-of-factly. 'I'm working with Ethan on the computer and the book will be finished in plenty of time. Luckily, even if we're snowed in, the manuscript can still be sent electronically.' She smiled at Celia. 'And the photos as well, if needs be, so there's no problem.'

Celia scowled at Amy across the table. 'I thought you were going home tomorrow?'

'So did I,' Amy said. She looked at Ethan and caught a glimpse of something in his eyes that made her breath catch. 'But a girl can change her mind.'

'I like this house,' George said suddenly. 'I don't want you to sell it, Dad.'

'Don't interrupt, George,' Celia said spitefully. 'You're obviously too young to eat with the adults, so I think you should go to bed now. This is a private matter between me and your father.'

'Then perhaps we should talk privately when dinner is over,' Ethan said mildly. He looked at his son. 'Finish your dinner, George, and on Christmas Eve we'll go and dig up the Christmas tree.' He looked round the table. 'It'll be hard work in the snow, so we'll need all the help we can get.'

'We'll all go,' Felix said. 'The book should be finished by then, so we'll make a party of it.'

6

George went to bed as soon as dinner was over. Mrs Peacock had gone home, Cathy was playing cards with Felix, and Angela was reading. Ethan and Celia were closeted in the study, and when Amy walked past the door she couldn't hear any shouting or breaking furniture, so she took that as a good sign. She gave George ten minutes to wash and get into bed, and then went quietly up the stairs.

By this time in the evening, some of the heat from the downstairs fires had risen to the top of the house, but the little boy's bedroom was still freezing cold. She wondered how any mother could leave a child to get into bed by himself, and then not even come upstairs to tuck him in.

'Are you still awake, George?' she whispered.

A muffled voice came from under the duvet and she walked further into the room.

'I brought cake,' she said. She remembered her mother saying those exact same words when she had been sent to bed early for doing something naughty. Except George hadn't done anything naughty. He had been sent to bed for having an opinion and, as far as Amy was concerned, that was not on.

His face appeared from under the covers. 'Mum sent me to bed because she doesn't like me interrupting.'

'You weren't interrupting,' Amy said. 'No one else was talking at the time, and someone has to be talking for you to be able to interrupt them. Here, have some cake.' She balanced the plate on the rumpled duvet, broke off a piece of chocolate cake, and popped it into his mouth. 'Chocolate is good for you, did you know that? It releases something inside you that makes you feel better.' She watched him eat without the slightest pang of guilt. Chocolate might

be murder on the teeth, but it was far better than feeling miserable.

'Will dad have to sell this house?'

'Not if he can help it. I expect your mother and father will work something out between them.'

'I like staying here.' He took another bite of cake and licked his fingers. 'I hate boarding school. The other boys, they put things in my bed.'

'Things?' Amy said worriedly. 'Like what?'

'A frog — and a wet sponge. The frog wasn't so bad, not once I realised what it was, but the wet sponge . . . ' he swallowed. 'The other kids thought I wet the bed.'

Amy wanted to cry for him. Ordinary day school was bad enough sometimes, but then you could go home and get a hug. She wondered how many hugs George got. Celia didn't look like a hugging kind of person.

She got a flannel from the bathroom and gave it to him to wipe his face and hands. 'Make sure you don't leave any

evidence, or we'll both be in trouble.' He climbed out of bed so she could shake the bed covers. 'Chocolate cake is not good to sleep on. Better than a frog or a wet sponge, but still not good.'

He giggled and snuggled down in bed, and then his head popped up again and he looked at her curiously. 'Are you the other woman?'

Amy was speechless for a moment. 'Who said anything about another woman?'

'Mum said dad must have one 'cos he looks happy, and I thought it might be you.'

'No, it's not me. Really, it's not. Your dad hasn't got another woman as far as I know.'

'I wouldn't mind if it was you.' George gave her a cheeky grin. 'As long as you bring me chocolate cake in bed.'

Had that got anything to do with Celia's request for more money, Amy wondered as she left the room. Was the demand for more money out of spite, rather than necessity, because she thought Ethan had found someone else? Thank

goodness it was Felix who had caught her kissing Ethan. She didn't want to add any more fuel to Celia's fire.

She went slowly down the stairs thinking about a little boy who was far too young for boarding school; a little boy who got things put in his bed, and had no one to hug him and tell him tomorrow wouldn't be so bad.

The study was empty and she entered the drawing room with trepidation, not sure what sort of atmosphere she would find. She had been right to be cautious. Ethan was standing in front of the fire with a scowl on his face and a drink in his hand, while Felix lounged on the sofa, long legs stretched in front of him. Otherwise the room was empty.

Felix looked up as Amy came into the room.

'Lots of big black clouds in here,' he said. 'Are you sure you wouldn't rather go to bed?'

Amy walked over to Ethan. 'What happened?'

'She threatened to take away my visiting rights with George and Molly.'

'If you don't increase her allowance?'

He nodded. 'Felix doesn't think she has a leg to stand on, but it's a worry. Ironically, I'm paying her enough to employ the best lawyers, and social services are always on the side of the mother when it comes to the children.'

'But she doesn't even like them,' Amy blurted.

Ethan burst out laughing. 'You're right, she doesn't, does she? I never really thought about it before. She dumps them on somebody else whenever she gets the chance but, for some reason, she doesn't want me to have them.'

'Because she thinks you've got another woman?' Amy said.

Both men stared at her.

'I went upstairs to say goodnight to George, and he asked me if I was the other woman. His mother evidently thinks you're having an affair because you look happy.'

'Do I?' He smiled, and Amy wanted to kiss him again. He looked down at his hands. 'I haven't had any pain all evening and I only took two paracetamol. Perhaps the red wine helps.'

'Or the other woman,' Felix said with a grin. 'Anyway, I'm glad you're feeling better, Ethan. Don't let Celia get to you. She'll bleed you dry if you let her.' He yawned. 'I'm going to bed. Don't do anything I wouldn't.'

Amy watched Felix leave the room and thought it would be sensible if she followed him. But she didn't.

'Have a drink with me,' Ethan said. 'It's really sad when a man has to drink alone. Besides, as my ex-wife said, you make me happy.'

Amy shook her head, taking the glass of wine he handed her. 'No, that was the other woman.'

When he didn't speak, she looked up at him, and barely had time to put down her glass before he pulled her into his arms. His kiss was unexpected and absolutely electrifying. She felt her

knees buckle, which only resulted in him pulling her closer. She wasn't quite sure how her fingers became entangled in his hair, or how her feet left the floor, but she came to her senses long enough to wrench her mouth from his and say his name.

'Ethan!'

He lowered her to the ground with a bemused expression on his face. 'Amy, I'm so sorry.'

'Please don't apologise,' she said more sharply than she had intended. 'If you tell me that kiss was accidental, rather than intentional, I shall be really disappointed. I stopped you because I was afraid your wife might walk in on us, not because I didn't enjoy every minute of it.'

His eyes twinkled. 'You've just become the other woman.'

'Exactly, and if Celia found out she'd use it as a weapon against you. You know she would.'

He handed Amy back her glass of wine and poured another for himself. 'I

don't know quite what that was, Amy. It might just have been a combination of paracetamol and red wine, but it felt like a bolt of lightening, and it definitely needs exploring further, don't you think?'

'Only not here, Ethan, not in this house. Not with Celia trying to find a reason to make you give her sole custody of Molly and George.' She looked deep into his warm brown eyes and took a breath. 'We'll finish the book tomorrow if we start early enough — and then I think I had better go home.'

He looked so devastated she almost changed her mind, but then she thought how much the little boy upstairs needed his father, and the fact that she would only have to look at Ethan to give the game away.

'We can meet after Christmas,' she said. 'If you still want to see me I shall be in London, and we can meet in the City. By then your book will be published and, hopefully, your lawyer

will have sorted out Celia's demand for more money. You can't let her blackmail you, Ethan. If you do, it won't ever stop. She'll hold custody of the children over your head like Damocles' sword.'

He took her hand. 'I don't want you to go, Amy. I want you to stay and help me dig up a tree, and be here on Christmas morning, and take George chocolate cake when he's sad.'

Her eyes opened wide. 'How did you know?'

'I followed you upstairs after Celia left. I was going to see George myself and tuck him up in bed, but you beat me to it. I listened outside the door.' He regarded her soberly. 'I probably shouldn't say this as it might frighten you away, but Molly and George need someone like you. Celia may have given birth to my children, and maybe she loved them once, but she gets bored very easily.' He sighed. 'She had a little dog when I met her, one you could fit in a handbag because that was fashionable at the time, but the poor little thing

only lasted six months, then she gave it away.'

'It's a pity she won't give the children away,' Amy said darkly. 'If you're semi-retired, you'd have time to look after them, and they could go to a local school. They need a permanent home, and all this house needs is central heating and better plumbing.'

She looked around with a dreamy expression on her face. 'Everything else should stay just as it is. You could restore the kitchen back to the way it should be, with quarry tiles and a wooden table everyone can sit round; somewhere for the kids to do their homework, and where all of you can eat and play. A proper family room.' She laughed self-consciously. 'I should definitely go, before I rearrange your life and your home.'

He smiled at her. 'I could live with that. I don't want to give up this house, but it might come to that, and the children will always come first. If we can get the book finished tomorrow, I'll

run you into the village myself the next day. That's Christmas Eve, but at least you'll get home in time for the celebrations.'

Amy couldn't imagine what she'd be celebrating. Ethan, with his house and his children, had somehow captured her heart, and she didn't want to leave any more than he wanted her to go. But she knew if she stayed it would only cause trouble, and she didn't want to be responsible for Ethan selling his house.

She slept fitfully, getting out of bed in the middle of the night to fetch another blanket from the cupboard. Eventually, she drifted off, and was still deeply asleep when Cathy banged on her bedroom door.

She called 'Come in,' and the events of the previous evening came rushing back. Had Ethan really kissed her, or had she dreamt it? She sat up with a start. The book had to be finished today and there was still a lot of work to do.

Then she had to go home.

Cathy put a cup of tea on the bedside

table and dropped down on the bed beside Amy. 'Guess what?'

Amy took a couple of sips of hot tea to clear her head. 'What?'

Cathy laughed, bouncing on the bed. 'I know I shouldn't be happy, because my mum can't get here, and it means you won't be able to go home, but there's so much of it Uncle Ethan thinks it's still going to be here on Christmas Day, and that's never happened before.'

Amy shook her head. 'I don't know what you're talking about.'

Cathy jumped off the bed and pulled back the heavy curtains. 'Just look out of the window. It snowed all night and it looks absolutely beautiful out there.'

Amy grabbed her robe and padded across the freezing floor in her bare feet. The ground had never properly thawed since their visit to Norwich, and the fresh snow had settled as soon as it touched. There looked to be at least a foot of it over everything, with the tall fir trees sagging under the weight and

icicles hanging like Christmas decorations from the eaves. The silence was absolute, with not a single creature or bird in sight. The terrace and lawns had merged into one, with no boundaries, and white hillocks dotted over the estate could be concealing anything from a large bush to a small car. Even as she looked, more fluffy white flakes started to fall.

Amy padded back across the bedroom, turning on the electric fire as she went, and slipped back into bed. She cupped the warm mug of tea in her hands and waited for her feet to thaw. Ethan was right, this was never going to go away by tomorrow.

Cathy was still grinning as she went out the door. 'It looks like you might be stuck here, after all.'

When Amy got downstairs the house was so quiet it seemed to be wrapped in a blanket of silence. It wasn't until she got near the kitchen that she heard voices. The smell of bacon cooking drew her in and she found Angela

already at the hob, turning rashers with her left hand. She had eventually agreed to have her arm in a sling to rest her wrist, and the swelling was beginning to go down, but she wouldn't be able to use the computer keyboard for some weeks.

'Where is everyone?' Amy asked.

Angela looked up. 'Can you break half a dozen eggs into a bowl for me, please. For some reason I find it impossible to do that with my left hand. In answer to your question, Ethan and Felix are trying to free one of the doors to the outside world. Felix had to climb through a window to get out, because the doors have so much snow against them they won't open. Mrs Peacock and Nick haven't turned up for obvious reasons, and because Celia is still in bed, Cathy has gone to get the children up and make sure they get dressed and clean their teeth.'

She paused for breath and slid the bacon into a metal dish. 'Can you pop that on the hotplate to keep warm while

I do the eggs. We could have had cereal, but all that snow has made me hungry, and the men will be starving, so bacon, eggs, and toast are on the menu.'

Amy got bread out of the freezer to thaw and set butter and marmalade on the table, and by the time the men arrived, smothered in flakes of soft snow, breakfast was ready. Cathy came in a few minutes later with a couple of still sleepy-looking children in tow, and everyone sat down at the table.

'The kitchen door is the only one we could clear,' Ethan said, 'so that'll have to do for now.'

'Where's mummy?' Molly asked, rubbing her eyes with her knuckles.

'Missing her breakfast,' George said with a grin. He looked at his father. 'Do we dig up the tree today?'

Ethan shook his head. 'Not today. I have to work with Amy today to finish the book. Tomorrow is Christmas Eve, and that's the day we dig up the tree.' He glanced out of the window. 'If we can find one in all this snow.' He looked

fondly at his little daughter. 'I'll have to carry you, Molly, or you might disappear in a drift of snow and never be seen again.'

She giggled happily, her missing mother obviously forgotten. 'Can I have a piggyback so I don't fall in the snow, daddy?'

Ethan laughed, and getting up from the table he plucked Molly out of her chair and swung her up on to his shoulders. 'I think we should practice round the house first, before we go out in the snow.'

As Molly's giggles disappeared into the distance Amy and Angela started to clear the table. Cathy and George went into the sitting room to find a jigsaw puzzle, and Felix picked up the log basket.

'I'll get some more logs before it snows any more.' He stopped beside Amy and put a hand on her shoulder. 'Celia's right. You do make him happy.'

Angela looked at Amy's pink face curiously. 'Is something going on I

should know about?'

Amy smiled. 'Nothing you should know about, not yet, anyway.' She looked at Angela seriously. 'Is it possible to fall in love in just a couple of weeks? Or is it just being close to him all the time that makes me feel like this? I don't know what's real anymore. But I do know we have to protect the children, and that means Celia mustn't suspect anything is going on. Not that it is,' she added hastily, 'but Celia already thinks there's another woman, and I don't want her to think it's me.'

'Even if it is,' Angela said dryly. 'Fair enough, Amy, but don't hurt him, will you? I love Ethan almost as much as . . . ' she stopped, flustered, and Amy finished the sentence for her.

'Almost as much as Felix. Yes, I know, and you should do something about that. Felix is in love with you, but he needs to know your rules, so explain them to him.'

'I have tried.'

'Not hard enough,' Amy said with a

smile. 'I have to find Ethan, and then we have to get the book finished and off to the publisher.'

'I'm sorry,' Angela said. 'I should be helping.'

'Help keep the children happy so he doesn't worry about them. Celia will be only too pleased if you take them off her hands for the day.'

Talk of the devil, Amy thought, as she walked into the study to find Celia sitting in front of the fire.

7

Amy looked at Ethan's ex-wife and decided it must take her half the morning to look like she did. She was wearing wide-legged trousers in a shade of deep plum, topped with a pale lavender sweater that had to be cashmere. High heeled boots decked her small feet, and Amy winced for the wood flooring.

'I was waiting for Ethan,' Celia said. 'But you'll have to do. I was going to ask him how you're going to get home, as we seem to be snow bound. Surely a snow-plough or something could be used to clear the lanes.'

'I'm sure it could,' Amy said. 'If it were deemed necessary.' She wondered why being in the same room with Celia made her talk like a schoolteacher. 'But I don't think the local council would consider me important enough to

launch a rescue operation.'

Celia sighed audibly. 'You realise you'll be in the way, don't you? Ethan won't want you here on Christmas Day with the rest of his family.'

'Perhaps you should ask me about that,' Ethan said from the doorway. Amy gave him a warning look, but he completely ignored her. 'When Angela was injured, Amy stayed to help me. It isn't her fault she's stranded here, and I'm sure, given the choice, she'd rather be with her own family at Christmas, so I suggest we all make her welcome.'

Annoyed at being put in the wrong, Celia got to her feet. 'Maybe it will thaw today.' She gave Amy a spiteful look. 'You never know your luck.'

She didn't exactly slam the door, that wasn't Celia's style, but without anyone to stop its progress, the heavy wooden door thudded home with a resounding thump.

'I hope that made her happy,' Ethan remarked. He turned and looked at Amy with such intensity she had to sit

down. 'Did I dream what happened yesterday?'

She smiled up at him. 'Do you mean, did you kiss me, and did I kiss you back? No, of course it didn't really happen, Ethan. You must have dreamt it.'

He caught her hands and pulled her to her feet. 'I'm going to have to check and find out what the real thing feels like, then. I'm going to need some sort of comparison before I can be sure last night was just a dream.'

Amy put both hands on his chest. 'Don't, Ethan. What if Celia comes back — or one of the children walks in?'

Pulling her into his arms he pressed his back against the door. 'Now no one can take us by surprise.'

'We have to work, Ethan,' Amy murmured, trying to avoid his mouth. 'You promised you'd wait until after Christmas.'

He kissed her soundly and then held her at arms length. 'Did I? I don't

remember saying anything like that. I promised to keep my other woman a secret, but that has nothing to do with kissing you. Which, incidentally, proves last night wasn't just a dream.'

'Work,' Amy said again, freeing herself from his embrace and backing to the other side of the desk. 'If you don't finish the book Celia will take all your money, and then I'll lose interest in you.'

He laughed out loud. 'That's a good incentive to get me back behind the computer.' He walked across the room and pulled up a chair next to her. 'Move over, then, and let's get some work done.'

A few minutes later the door opened and Celia walked back in. She looked surprised to find them sitting at the computer.

'I thought I heard you laugh, Ethan, but I must have been mistaken. You don't do that, do you?' She studied them for a moment. 'Wouldn't two computer screens be more sensible than

both of you working on one? It looks a bit too cosy, if you ask me.'

'I'm not asking you, Celia, and I am extremely busy, so was there something you wanted.'

'When Angela brings the morning coffee, I've asked her to bring an extra cup so I can sit and chat to you both. There's no point in us all congregating in different rooms in the house.'

Amy had kept silent, but she could see what Celia was doing. Interrupt Ethan enough, and he wouldn't get the book finished.

'We're not taking a coffee break today, Celia. We both have too much to do.' She stared at Celia expectantly until the woman reluctantly opened the door again. 'And it might be best if you left Ethan in peace for a couple of hours. We'll be in the kitchen for lunch later on if you're really that desperate for company.'

'I know she deserves everything she gets,' Ethan said with a smile as Celia left the room, 'but I'm beginning to feel

126

quite sorry for her.'

The last draft of the book had already been finished to Amy's satisfaction, and it was now just a case of going over the whole thing to make sure there were no glaring errors. Amy printed out the text and gave it to Ethan to read by the fire, while she checked the positioning of the photos and their captions on the computer screen. By lunchtime they had finished checking the manuscript and were both feeling elated

'Let's stop now,' Ethan said. 'I'm hungry.'

Amy nodded. She was feeling tired but happy. They had proved that whatever chemistry there was between them didn't affect their work, and she hoped he'd ask for her help again with his second book. 'It's almost done,' she said, 'and once we know it's reached the publishers, we can really celebrate.'

He gave her a quick kiss. 'Champagne it is, then. I shall be opening the last case, so let's hope the snow doesn't keep up much longer.'

Amy looked at him soberly. 'If it thaws I shall be going home, Ethan. I have to, for everyone's sake.' She left the room before he could say anything, and headed for the kitchen. Come to think of it, she was feeling hungry as well.

She had expected to find Celia already in the kitchen, but there was no sign of her. Both children were sitting at the table with plates in front of them while Cathy sliced ham and Angela fussed with a deep fat fryer.

'I know exactly what to do with a pan of oil and a chip basket, but this thing is electric and I can't see the chips. How am I supposed to know when they're done?'

Felix stopped buttering bread to stand beside her. 'If you've set the dial properly it will buzz when the chips are ready.' At that moment a buzzer sounded. He put his arm round Angela's shoulders and gave her a little squeeze. 'See? Nothing to worry about.'

'Let me take over buttering the bread

while you and Angela dish up, Felix,'
Amy said. 'I feel guilty for not getting
here earlier. I keep forgetting, with Mrs
Peacock stranded at home, there's no
one to cook for us.'

'Not a problem.' Felix looked up as
Ethan walked in. 'Book finished?'

Ethan smiled. He looked, Amy
thought, as if a weight had been lifted
from his shoulders. There was no
inflammation in his fingers, as far as she
could see, and he seemed completely
relaxed.

'Almost finished, thanks to Amy.
We're sending it off electronically later
today.' He helped himself to ham as
Angela dished up a bowl of perfect
chips.

'Wow,' she said. 'Technology has its
advantages, after all.

They had almost finished their meal
before Celia appeared. She looked pink
and flustered, but also, Amy thought,
strangely satisfied. Like a cat who had
just finished a large bowl of cream.

'Ethan,' she said dramatically, 'I think

I've ruined your book. I'm so sorry. I don't know what to say.' She looked around the room as if expecting sympathy. 'It was a complete accident.'

Ethan frowned at her, but didn't get up from the table, and Amy felt her heart sink. This is what Celia did to him. She waited until he was on a high and then gave a little tug at the rug beneath his feet. Just enough to topple him. There was an air of expectancy about her and a glint of excitement in her eyes, like a hunter about to shoot a deer.

'What have you done, Celia?' he asked resignedly.

Celia bit her lip and did her best to look contrite. 'I only wanted to read your book, Ethan. You never show me your work, and I knew it was going off to the publishers. I was sitting in the study with a cup of coffee, reading the printout you'd left on your desk, when my cup slipped and I tipped coffee all over the manuscript. I've ruined it.'

'That won't be a problem, Celia,'

Amy said. 'We have it all saved on to the computer hard drive. I'll just print out another copy.'

Celia smiled, 'I'm so glad, because you're right, it's really good. The computer had been left on, so after I spilt the coffee I started reading the book on the monitor, but then I realised it was lunch time.' She smiled at Ethan. 'I thought it was silly to leave the computer on when no one was in the office, so when I left I turned it off for you.'

'That's OK,' Ethan said warily. 'As long as you didn't touch anything. We've almost finished editing the book.'

'Oh, I didn't touch any of the keys,' Celia said brightly. 'But a little box came up asking if I wanted to save any changes, and I hadn't made any, so I said no.'

There was complete silence. Even the two children stared at their mother without saying a word. If Celia had been relying on a dramatic climax she had achieved her aim. All the work

Ethan and Amy had done on the manuscript during the morning had just been deleted.

'The recycle bin,' Amy said. 'It will be in there, won't it?'

Celia beamed at them. 'While I was at it, I emptied that for you as well.' Seeing Amy's expression, she opened her eyes wide and put a hand to her mouth. 'I didn't do anything wrong, did I? Ethan told me all the stuff in the bin is just trash.'

Ethan looked at Amy and she dropped her eyes. She couldn't look at him. This was the ultimate betrayal. There was no way Celia could have deleted their work by accident, she ran a business, and even if they could rescue the typescript, Celia knew there wasn't time to put all their changes back on the computer, and finish checking the manuscript, before the deadline ran out at the end of the day. From tomorrow, the publishing house would be closed down for the Christmas holidays.

'You're not that stupid, Celia,' Felix said in disgust. 'What you did was quite deliberate.'

'How can you say that?' Celia managed to force out real tears. 'I told you it was an accident.'

'Perhaps if we all worked on it,' Angela suggested. 'I'm sure we can clean up the printed copy enough to read it.'

Ethan looked at Amy again. 'I think Celia's done enough, don't you? There's no point in doing any more work on the book now, is there?'

She looked back at him thoughtfully for a moment, and then shook her head. 'No point at all.'

'Is there any thing I can do to help?' Celia asked. She was sitting at the table cuddling Molly, who was looking completely bewildered by her mother's sudden show of affection. 'I feel too upset to eat.'

'Stay with Cathy and the children,' Ethan told her. 'We don't need your help, but we do need time to sort out

what to do next. I might try emailing the publisher to see if they will give me extra time.'

'They won't,' Amy said flatly. 'They already told you that.'

Without saying another word, he marched out of the room. Amy beckoned to Felix and Angela, and they all followed Ethan into the study. Amy shut the door and was about to say something, when Ethan put a finger to his lips. He put his ear to the crack in the door, listened for a minute, and then pulled it open. Celia almost fell into the room.

'Did you want something?' he asked coldly. 'If not, perhaps you could leave us alone to sort out the mess you've made. You've done your best to sabotage my work, Celia, and I'll never forgive you for that. I also want you to know that if I can find any way to take Molly and George away from you, I will.'

Just for a second Amy thought she saw a flicker of fear in Celia's eyes, and

then Ethan slammed the door in her face. He looked at the three of them soberly for a moment, and then his face split into a wide grin.

'Have you still got it, Amy?'

She reached for the gold chain round her neck and pulled it free. Hanging from the chain was a small memory stick. 'Yes, it's still here.' She turned to Felix and Angela. 'We both had a feeling Celia might try to sabotage the book, so we took precautions, but Ethan wants her to think she succeeded. That way we might get through Christmas without any more dramas.'

Angela laughed. 'So you saved the whole book on to a memory stick?'

Amy nodded. 'The manuscript has had its final edit, and it's all ready to go, so all I have to do is email it to the publishers. Ethan's already written the covering letter.'

She turned the computer back on while Ethan pulled a large box from behind the desk. He opened the box and took out a bottle of champagne. 'I

was going to save this for Christmas Day, but I think we deserve a glass right now.'

Amy swung the desk chair round. 'It's done,' she said with a smile. She noticed Ethan was having trouble with the champagne cork and took the bottle from him. 'I'm good at this,' she said, twisting off the cage. 'You just have to remember not to point the bottle at anything breakable.'

Angela looked at Ethan thoughtfully. 'I've noticed you have a problem with your hands, Ethan. Felix and Amy both seem to know all about it, so when were you thinking of telling me?'

Ethan looked shamefaced. 'I'm sorry, Angela. Amy recognised my rheumatoid arthritis because her mother has it, and Felix has known for a while. I've had to give up my position at the hospital. That's why the book is so important. I can only do consultancy work now, so I'm going to need another source of income, and if the publishers find out I'm no longer a practicing surgeon, they

might cancel my contract.'

Angela hugged him. 'I'm so sorry, Ethan. I know you would have told me in the end, and you're right, the fewer people who know about it, the better. Celia would have a field day with something like that.' She looked at his hands. 'I've noticed your fingers are swollen sometimes, but they look fine today.'

He held his hands up in front of his face. 'It seems to be partly stress related.' Smiling at Amy, he said, 'And I seem to be fairly stress free at the moment.'

The cork coming out of the bottle saved Amy's blushes. She filled four glasses and they toasted the book, which was hopefully now winging its way to London, and then Angela and Felix left the study with a promise not to tell Celia anything.

As soon as they had gone, Ethan poured out the last of the champagne.

'This is just for us,' he said. 'I couldn't have done this without you,

Amy. I know we've only just met, but I think I'm falling in love with you.' As she put down her drink in shocked amazement, he took her hands in his. 'Please tell me if I'm making an absolute fool of myself. I'm older than you.' He smiled. 'Not quite old enough to be your father, but still quite a lot older, and as an out of work surgeon I'm not a very good catch at the moment.'

She started to say something but he pressed a finger against her lips.

'While I'm on a roll, you might as well hear me out. Celia will do all she can to destroy any relationship we might have, and the children are always going to be a problem. I can't give them up, Amy, and I'm going to get full custody if I possibly can. That isn't fair on you. Neither is this mausoleum of a house, but I won't give that up either. So if you want to take off as soon as the snow thaws, and never see me again, I won't stop you. You'd have good reason.'

'Have you finished?' she asked, when he stopped for breath. 'Because if so you can shut up and listen to me. I don't care how old you are. I worked it out and I think you're thirteen years older than me, which is nothing, and definitely not old enough to be my father, unless you were a particularly precocious child. I am prepared to lock swords with Celia any time she wants to take me on, and I think your children like me, but that's probably because I'm a much nicer person than their mother. And I love your house. There are a few things that would have to change before I could live here permanently, like the plumbing and heating, but otherwise it just needs a little love and attention, and that doesn't only apply to the house.' She smiled at him. 'I think I love you, too, Ethan, so why don't you try and convince me.'

He pulled her into his arms and leant his back against the door again. 'Be careful what you wish for, Amy Franklin.'

A few moments later she released herself from his embrace. 'If Celia finds out about us, she'll ruin everyone's Christmas, and I don't want to be responsible for that. Enjoy the celebrations with your family and treat me as an unwanted guest which, as far as your ex-wife is concerned, I am.' She reached up to kiss him on the cheek. 'We have the rest of our lives to be together, if that's what we want, and I know everything else will sort itself out in the end. It always does.'

He smiled at her. 'I don't know whether I'm going to be able to cope with all this eternal optimism for the rest of my life. I'd just got used to being miserable.'

8

The next morning Amy awoke to find sunshine streaming in through a crack in the curtains. For a moment she couldn't think why she felt so happy, and then things started to come back to her. The book had been finished inside the deadline in spite of Celia's sabotage plan, Ethan had said he loved her, and today was Christmas Eve.

She hardly felt the cold as she climbed out of the big bed and turned on the fire. She decided to have a bath, and it was almost ready when she heard Cathy knock on the door with her tea.

'Goodness,' the girl said. 'You're awake early. You've done me out of my job of filling your bath.' She waited while Amy got back into bed and then sat down beside her. 'Why do you look so happy? You should be all upset because you can't go home.'

'I'm making the best of things,' Amy said. 'I'm sure Christmas here will be much more fun than Christmas in London. There's snow still on the ground, and Ethan is going to dig up a tree and — I don't know — everything just seems perfect all of a sudden.'

'Good for you,' Cathy said. 'You're right, sometimes you just have to sit back and enjoy whatever happens. If Mrs Peacock could have got here she'd be cooking all sorts of wonderful things, so us girls have to spend all day in the kitchen making mince pies and trifles, and I think that's going to be fun. Felix got the turkeys out of the freezer a couple of days ago, and everything else we need, like cranberry sauce and stuff, is around somewhere. We just have to find it.'

'A sort of food hunt,' Amy said, sipping her tea. 'Is Celia going to help with the cooking?'

Cathy laughed. 'I doubt it. But the children want to help, which could be interesting. Molly told me she can make

jam tarts, and George says he's good at licking mixing bowls clean. I bet my mum taught them how to do that. Hopefully, Ethan will take them to dig up the tree and leave us girls in peace.'

Amy got out of bed and wrapped herself in her robe before she froze to death. 'Is your mum upset at not being able to get here?'

Cathy shrugged. 'Not really. She's got loads of friends who'll invite her round for Christmas dinner. The phone lines are down, but I spoke to her on my mobile phone, and she's fine. It will be one Christmas she doesn't have to look after Molly and George all day.'

After Cathy had gone, Amy had a quick bath and dressed in jeans and a long-sleeved sweater. She hoped some-one had an apron to lend her if she was supposed to cook. She wasn't the tidiest of people in a kitchen. She had learnt the hard way when her mother had a bad day and couldn't hold a spoon. There was never enough money for a take-away, so Amy often had to

improvise, conjuring up a meal from anything she could find in the fridge. She was a dab hand at making an omelette, and if there was dried pasta around she could rustle up a mean macaroni cheese.

A full Christmas dinner, however, was another matter altogether.

Angela, as usual, was already in the kitchen wielding a frying pan of sizzling bacon. Amy took over breaking eggs into a bowl without being asked, and when Felix arrived a few minutes later he started on the toast. Ethan came into the kitchen behind his friend and set himself the task of laying the table.

'We make a good team, don't we?' Angela said. 'Celia still in bed?'

When no one answered, she laughed. 'None of us really care, do we? She's useless in the kitchen.'

'She's useless most places,' Ethan said. 'She's a useless housewife and mother, and her decorating business is evidently going downhill. That's why she's trying to get more money out of

me. I don't know why it took me so long to realise what she's really like.'

'Because you only see the good in people,' Amy said. She looked at her bowl of eggs. 'Shall I scramble these now, or do we wait for Cathy and the children?'

Felix started buttering toast. 'Let's eat. This is a grown-up breakfast. We can do some eggy-bread for the kids later on. We're going to have to look really gutted when we see Celia, so we might as well be cheerful while we can.'

They saved some bacon for Cathy, and a few minutes later she appeared with Celia and the children. 'I've decided I should spend time with the children, as it's Christmas Eve,' Celia said, 'so I'm going with them to help dig up the tree.'

As soon as everyone had been fed, the dishes cleared away, and the dishwasher filled, Cathy helped Celia dress the children for the cold. The sun had gone and it had started snowing again. Celia was wearing a fur-lined

145

jacket with jeans tucked into high leather boots. The boots were flat-heeled for once. The children had rubber boots over two pairs of socks, and Cathy pulled on their mittens and wrapped scarves around their necks.

'Keep warm,' she said, dropping a kiss on Molly's head as Celia stood impatiently in the open doorway.

As soon as the tree-finding party had disappeared into the snow, the children whooping with excitement, Angela sat down at the table with a notebook and pen.

'I was thinking of making some sort of a rota,' she said. 'As the men have taken the children with them to dig up the tree, we can get on with the cooking, but I think we need some sort of a system, or we'll be falling over one another.'

'Four women in a kitchen together?' Amy shook her head. 'You could be right.'

'Don't include Celia,' Angela said. 'Because she's got out of the cooking

yet again, and she'd be more trouble than she's worth. I think we can manage without her, don't you, girls.'

'Mum and Mrs Peacock bought everything for Christmas dinner weeks ago,' Cathy said. 'All except the fresh vegetables, and there's plenty of frozen sprouts and things in the freezer.'

'Hands up anyone who likes sprouts.' Angela looked for a show of hands and found none. 'Right then, if no one likes sprouts, there's no point in cooking them. Sprouts are off the menu. We'll substitute peas.'

A lot of substitutes were made during the course of the morning. Sometimes because no one wanted that particular item of food on their plate or, more often, because no one knew how to cook it. Homemade Christmas puddings had been found in the larder and mince pies in the freezer. Angela thought she knew what to do with the frozen cranberries to make sauce, and Amy volunteered to make the trifle.

'Put enough sherry in,' she said, 'and

nobody cares what else is in it.'

She found packets of sponge fingers to soak in sherry and a jar of bottled raspberries to put in the jelly. The big tubs of fresh cream were still within their sell by date, and she could hear custard sloshing in a tin. She was having the most fun for years. It really was fate, she reasoned, that had made her stay. If she had gone home when she intended Ethan would never have told her how he felt about her, and they might never have seen one another again.

Lunch was going to be soup and a box of recently discovered cheese crackers, with assorted cheeses and pickles, followed by chocolate chip cookies that Cathy had attempted, but not quite succeeded, in baking. Taken out of the oven a fraction too soon, they had spread over the baking tray to twice the size they should have been.

Just as they were clearing the table for lunch, Ethan appeared in a flurry of snow, closely followed by Felix.

'We left the tree outside because it's too big to get in the house at the moment. I'm going to have to chop the top off.' Ethan smiled as he looked round the kitchen. 'You've made a bit of a mess, haven't you? Celia won't be pleased.'

Amy looked round Celia's designer kitchen guiltily. They had made a mess. The sink was full of dirty dishes ready to go in the dishwasher when the breakfast things came out, and large splodges of unknown origin dotted the work surfaces and the floor. She noticed something had settled on the hob and turned into a brown crust, a thin wisp of smoke still rising from its remains.

'Where is Celia?' she asked.

Ethan stopped in the middle of taking off his coat. 'She was bringing the children home. They left before us because Molly was getting cold. Haven't they come back yet?'

As Angela shook her head, Cathy said, 'Perhaps they came in the front

door and went straight upstairs.'

'The front door won't open,' Felix said slowly. 'It's blocked with snow.' He looked at Ethan. 'They must still be out there.'

Cathy pulled off her apron. 'I'll check the house.'

Amy put her hand on Ethan's arm as he struggled back into his coat. 'Wait until Cathy comes back, they may be in the house somewhere.'

He frowned at her. 'They can't have come in without any of you noticing. Not if you've been in the kitchen all the morning. It started to snow again, so I told Celia to bring them home. We were only about a hundred yards from the house; you could see it through the trees. I should have known she wouldn't be able to do something as simple as that without messing it up.'

Felix shrugged back into his own jacket and slipped his feet into his boots. 'I'll help you look for them, they can't be far away.'

Cathy burst back into the room.

'They're not in the house. I looked everywhere.'

Without a word Ethan pulled open the door and walked out into the snow. Felix stood for a minute in the doorway. 'You all stay here in case they come back. I've got my phone with me. I'll call you when we find them.'

'I'm worried about Molly,' Cathy said. 'If she's tired she'll want to be carried, and Celia won't do that. I wish I'd gone with them. Ethan should never have sent them back on their own.'

Angela looked out of the window. 'He trusted their mother to bring them home safely, more fool him. They must have been in that little spinney by the lake, that's where all the spruce trees grow.'

Amy joined Angela and Cathy at the window. 'I hope the children didn't go near the lake. The ice looks solid, but it isn't.'

'Look!' Angela pointed at someone staggering through the snow towards the house. 'It's Celia!'

Amy pulled the door open and rushed out to help Celia into the house. 'What happened?' she asked the shivering woman. 'Where are the children?'

'I don't know where they are.' Celia dropped into a chair and pulled down the hood of her jacket. Her face was bright red with cold and her long false eyelashes were dotted with ice. 'I looked and looked, but I couldn't find them.'

'How on earth did you lose them in the first place?' Angela asked in disbelief. 'You only had to bring them back to the house.'

'I needed a cigarette, so I sent them on ahead a little way because I didn't want George to tell his father I was still smoking.' She looked up at them appealingly. 'I didn't leave them on their own for more than a few minutes, but when I caught up with George he said Molly had run away from him and he couldn't find her. We called and called, but she didn't answer.'

'So where's George now?' Amy asked. This was like a scenario from a

nightmare. Surely the stupid woman hadn't left the nine-year-old alone again.

'I tried to make him come back with me, but he ran off to look for Molly.' Celia looked near to tears. 'I didn't know what to do, so I came back here.

'Felix and Ethan are already looking for the children. Exactly where did you leave George?'

'He said he was going to look down by the lake because Molly said she wanted to see the ducks. Molly had already asked Ethan to take her, but he said it was too cold.' Celia was crying now. 'It's Ethan's fault. If he'd taken Molly to see the ducks she wouldn't have run off like that.'

Amy took her mobile phone out of her apron pocket. 'I know you're upset, but you can't always blame other people, Celia.' She dialled Ethan's number but the phone went straight to voice mail. She tried Felix with the same result.

'They won't have a signal if they're in amongst the trees,' Celia mumbled. She

had a tissue pressed to her eyes and she was still shaking with cold, but no one was taking any notice of her.

'I'll have to go to the lake and find George,' Amy said. 'The men might not think to look there. All of you stay here in case the children come back, or the men phone to say they've found them. My phone should work by the lake, so ring me if anything happens.'

She ran upstairs to put on her warmest clothes as quickly as she could. There was no point in getting frozen to death, that way she'd be no help to anyone. As she left the house and started towards the lake, she had a picture of little Molly running out onto the ice to play with the ducks. Ethan had said the lake froze over every winter but it was never safe to walk on, and at the edges the ice was as thin and brittle as glass.

She reached the lake in record time, looking for footprints as she went, but the fresh snow was covering everything, her own footprints disappearing even as

she made them. She scanned the lake anxiously, looking for any breaks in the ice where a child might have fallen through. A couple of ducks skated towards her, thinking she might be a source of food, but she shooed them away. She started walking round the lake calling the children's names and after a moment she heard someone crashing through the bushes. Ethan ran towards her, his face screwed up with anxiety.

'What are you doing out here?' he said angrily. 'Felix told you to stay in the house.'

'I don't always do what I'm told, Ethan,' she answered sharply. 'That's something you're going to have to learn. Celia came back to the house, but I couldn't get you on the phone to tell you. She left the children by themselves while she had a cigarette, and Molly ran away from George. Celia thinks Molly came to the lake to see the ducks. That's why I'm here. I suggest we both go opposite ways round the

lake and see if we can find either of them.'

His eyes scanned the lake. 'No one's fallen in. The ice is unbroken.'

'I know.' She didn't have time to stand arguing with Ethan while his children froze to death. Molly was such a little thing and she had been out in the cold a long time.

Amy started round the lake again, still calling the children's names, and a few minutes later she heard a faint noise, not beside the lake, but off into the trees. She left the ice-covered water and headed towards the trees, not young spruce this time, but tall firs laden with snow. The frozen under-growth made walking difficult, but she called again and this time got a definite response. She found George squatting on the ground under a bush cradling Molly in his arms. His tears had frozen on his face and his lips were blue with cold.

The little girl looked at Amy sleepily, the cold making her drowsy, but her

colour was good.

'I found her,' George said, 'but she wouldn't walk, so I carried her as far as I could until she got too heavy.'

'You did really well,' Amy said. 'Carrying her kept you both warm, but you were right to stop when you did. If you'd become exhausted and gone to sleep, I might never have found you in time.'

She pulled her phone out of her pocket and called Ethan. He arrived a few moments later at a run, Felix not far behind. 'You have a very brave little boy,' Amy told Ethan. 'He found his little sister all by himself, then he kept her warm until we arrived. I think he deserves a medal.'

Ethan dropped to his knees on the snowy ground and hugged his children. 'I can do better than a medal,' he told George. 'How about you come and live with me for good? No more boarding school or summer camp ever again.'

Felix picked Molly up in his arms. 'I'll take her back to the house, Ethan.

She needs warming up. You bring George back with you.'

George was much too old to be carried, but he settled for a piggyback. 'Did you mean that, Dad?' he asked. 'Can I really live with you?'

'If you want to,' Ethan said. 'You might have to tell a judge that you'd rather be with me, and your mum might object, but you don't have to go back to boarding school, I promise you that, and you'll be able to see your mum whenever you want to.'

'Good,' George said contentedly. 'She might get lonely on her own.'

Molly recovered quickly after a warm bath and a change of clothes. George was probably the most chilled, and Amy worried about him for a little while, but food was all he needed to buck him up. Angela opened a tin of soup and warmed rolls in the microwave and the two children finished the lot. They were then sent to bed for a couple of hours while the grownups recovered.

Celia looked ghostly white and Amy

almost felt sorry for her.

'They nearly died, didn't they?' she said fearfully. 'What would have happened to me if they'd both died?'

'I'd have killed you,' Ethan said matter-of-factly. 'But I'll tell you what is going to happen, Celia. You're going to hand custody of the children over to me, otherwise I shall report you to the authorities for neglect. I'll give you access, but on my terms, and if you attempt to go against me on this I'll give the story to the newspapers.' He turned away from her contemptuously. 'You'd better put on some more soup, Angela. Celia is going to bed, but the rescue party is starving.'

9

Amy awoke on Christmas morning to a strange noise coming from the landing. She pulled on a robe and opened the bedroom door. The noise was coming from the main hall. Making sure no one was about, she crept over to the banisters and looked down. George suddenly appeared on a mountain bike and almost crashed into a large blue vase standing next to the front door. Before she could stop herself, Amy let out a little squeal, and George looked up. When he saw Amy his face split into a big grin.

'I got a bike,' he called up to her. 'Dad bought it for me to ride when I'm living here. I can't have a bike in London because of the traffic.' He did a little twirl on the back wheel, leaving a rubber mark on the polished floor. 'Isn't it great?'

Amy clutched her robe round her. 'Wonderful, but are you supposed to be riding a bike in the house?'

'Dad says it's OK if I'm careful. The snow is too deep to ride outside.'

That seemed perfectly logical so Amy went back into her room and shut the door. She must have overslept, she realised, because the cup of tea beside her bed was only just warm. Cathy must have crept in while she was still sleeping.

Amy had a quick wash, pulled on jeans and a sweater, and hurried down to the kitchen. The big room was warm and busy. Cathy was pouring cereal into a bowl for Molly, who looked completely recovered from her adventure, while Celia turned bacon slices in a pan. Angela was thawing bread in the microwave and transferring it to the toaster.

'It sticks if you put it in the toaster while it's still frozen,' she said by way of explanation.

Amy looked at Celia and raised a

questioning eyebrow. Cathy grinned. 'Penance,' she said. 'Everyone helps today, or no Christmas dinner.

Angela looked over from her place at the kitchen counter. 'We let you sleep in this morning. Yesterday's trauma was enough to make anyone tired.'

'I got a 'puter game,' Molly said, her mouth full of chocolate crispies, 'and a bear that speaks.'

'And a dolls pram from your daddy,' Celia said, smiling at her daughter. 'You must remember to thank him.' She turned to Amy. 'And I believe I have to thank you for finding the children yesterday. I know I shouldn't have left them out there on their own, but I've never pretended I was any good at parenting.' Turning her back on Amy, she picked up the tongs and started transferring the bacon to a dish. 'As you can see, they're fine this morning.'

There was very little sign of remorse, Amy noticed, but before she could answer, Ethan and Felix came into the kitchen and she busied herself helping

Angela dish up breakfast.

The morning passed in a flurry of activity. The children had been allowed to come downstairs and open their presents as soon as they woke up, but the grownups had to wait until late afternoon, when drinks were served in the drawing room prior to Christmas Dinner.

'We eat in the dining hall today,' Ethan said. 'A Christmas tradition ever since I bought the house. Felix helped me set the tree up in the hall last night, but it still needs decorating. We didn't have time to do it yesterday because we lost a couple of children in the snow.' He looked round the room. 'So who's going to help?'

Molly left her cereal to fling herself at her father's legs. 'Me. I can help.'

George arrived through the doors on his bike and skidded to a halt. 'No you can't, you're too short, you can't reach the branches.'

Molly started to sniffle and Ethan picked her up. 'If I hold her she can

reach,' he told George, 'so you can both help.'

He looked across the kitchen and smiled at Amy. She smiled back, hoping Celia didn't notice, but the woman had swung round at the sound of the bike, a frown creasing her usually smooth forehead. For a moment, Amy thought she was going to tell George off for marking the floor, but after hesitating a moment, Celia opened the oven door and pushed in the pan of bacon. 'Please be careful, George,' was all she said.

'Don't worry about the floor, George,' Ethan told his son. 'It's Christmas Day, and if you spoil the floor, I'll just have to replace it. I kept all the old quarry tiles, so it won't be a problem.'

Celia scowled at Ethan and then left the room without a word, but no one seemed particularly bothered. The children were told to go and play with their new toys until the grownups had finished their breakfast, and Cathy took a tray up to Celia in her room.

'It's worth it, just to get rid of her,'

Cathy said when she returned. 'She only eats toast and fruit, and makes everyone else feel guilty for enjoying a slice of bacon and some scrambled eggs.' She looked at Ethan. 'Your ex says she's got a headache, but she'll be down later.'

Felix looked at his friend and laughed. 'That's how she got out of helping last year, if I remember, and then we had Mrs Peacock cooking for us. Just imagine if Celia was asked to peel a potato.'

As soon as the men had left the kitchen the women started preparing the food. Most of the hard work had been done the day before, but the turkey still had to go in the oven.

'How long will it take?' Angela asked worriedly. 'It's a lot bigger than those chickens.'

Cathy pulled out her mobile phone. 'Hang on a minute and I'll ask mum. I want to wish her a happy Christmas, anyway.'

While Cathy was on the phone, Amy

decided to send a text to her own parents in Florida, and Angela did the same, sending a message to her mother in Italy. Amy tried to imagine what she would be doing if she was still in London. She would probably lie in bed until mid-morning, and then join some friends for drinks before Christmas lunch. The restaurant had been booked months ago, and she had been looking forward to the meal, but that didn't seem important any more. Her friends in London were really only acquaintances, she realised, compared with the warm companionship she felt here.

Angela opened the fridge and took out a bottle of wine. 'Ethan keeps his best wine locked up, but Mrs Peacock uses this for cooking, so I'm sure it's fine. I thought we might celebrate Ethan winning a round with Celia.' She smiled at Amy. 'He seems to have got a new lease of life from somewhere.'

They raised their glasses to wish Ethan good luck, and then decided they might as well finish the bottle and get

rid of the evidence before they left the kitchen. Amy found Felix and Ethan struggling to cope with two exuberant children and a pile of decorations that didn't seem to be diminishing, so Cathy took the children to play in the drawing room, while Amy and Angela helped the men finish decorating the tree. The magnificent spruce stood in a red tub and reached from the floor to the ceiling. When it was decked out in all its splendour, it looked spectacular, sparkling with gold and silver balls, and tiny coloured lights that flashed like fireflies among the branches.

The hall had been festooned with holly, a log fire burned in the hearth, and a CD of Christmas carols played softly in the background. Amy stood back to admire their work, and couldn't remember a time when she had been this happy.

'I've got champagne on ice,' Ethan said. 'Can you girls manage the food by yourselves, or do you want us to help?'

'We'll put everything in the hostess trolley before we go up to change,' Angela said. 'You and Felix make sure there are plenty of logs for the fires, and look after the drinks, we can manage the rest between us.'

Angela and Amy arranged to come downstairs early so they could set the table while Cathy got the children dressed for dinner. 'I doubt Celia will make an appearance until the food is on the table,' Cathy said. 'She has no idea how to look after those children. She has a full-time nanny, so she doesn't ever have to put them to bed or get them dressed in the morning.'

Amy went upstairs and had a leisurely bath before deciding what she was going to wear. She hoped the giving of presents round the tree wasn't going to be an embarrassment. If she had known she would be snowed in, she would have bought presents for everyone, but she had been sure she was going to be back in London long before Christmas Day. Next year, she told

herself happily, she would buy Ethan something special.

By the time she had finished her day dreaming, the bath water was cold, but she had turned on her little fire so she could stand in her underwear without freezing to death, and inspect her meagre wardrobe. She was just about to give up in despair when there was a knock on her bedroom door, and Cathy came in clutching an armful of clothes.

'I thought you might have a problem because we all dress up tonight, so I bought some of my things for you to try. Angela can't help because she's too tall and a size bigger than you.' Cathy stood back and looked Amy up and down. 'We're about the same size, I think.'

'But I'm ten years older than you.'

'And some of the dresses my mum buys me are ten years older than me as well. This might fit you, it just looks silly on me.' Cathy held up a pale blue confection with a staggered hemline and shoestring straps. 'Or this green

one. It makes me look like a tart.'

Amy laughed, but held the green dress against her and looked in the mirror. 'It's beautiful, Cathy. May I try it on?'

The dress was a sheath of emerald green jersey that clung in places and skimmed in others. Cathy was right; it was far too old for a teenager, but just perfect for someone who wanted to crush the opposition.

She did a twirl in front of the mirror and Cathy clapped.

'It looks great on you. Why didn't it look like that on me? I think my bottom must be bigger than yours.' She grinned. 'Celia will be jealous, and the men won't be able to stop looking at you. Ethan, anyway. I think Felix fancies Angela.' She held up a box. 'What size shoes do you take? I've got green ones to match the dress.'

Half an hour later Amy made her way carefully down the stairs in a borrowed dress and a pair of shoes that were a size too big, but she felt wonderful.

Cathy had helped style her hair with a pair of tongs, and her usually straight locks now fell in loose curls round her face. Lip-gloss and mascara were the only items of makeup she needed, but tonight she had added a hint of blusher and a dash of her favourite perfume. If Celia thought she was out to impress Ethan, Celia would be perfectly right.

'You look amazing,' Angela said, when Amy walked into the kitchen. 'But I think I look pretty amazing as well, so let's get the table set and go and knock their socks off.'

The two women walked into the drawing room together and got exactly the reaction they wanted. Open-mouthed admiration from both men.

Celia was already ensconced in a chair by the fire, her elegant legs crossed at the ankle, a cigarette in one hand and a glass of champagne in the other. 'My, my,' she said with a raised eyebrow. 'You both scrub up quite nicely when you really try.'

Cathy came in with the children and

once everyone was seated, George and Molly handed out the presents for the adults. Celia seemed pleased with the Prada handbag Ethan had given her, and got out of her chair to give him a quick peck on the cheek.

'It's a shame we don't have anything for you Amy, but we weren't expecting you to still be here.'

Ethan took a tiny package from his pocket. 'Actually, I do have something for you Amy. It's nothing much, just a small thank you for all the work you've done for me.' He looked at Celia. 'If it hadn't been for Amy, I would never have met the publisher's deadline.'

Celia looked at him in shocked amazement. 'But you didn't. You couldn't. I deleted the book from the computer. I made sure . . . ' She suddenly realised what she had said and tried to backtrack. 'I thought you'd lost the book for good.'

'I know you did,' he smiled at his ex-wife with satisfaction. 'At least you've admitted you did it deliberately.

Luckily Amy had saved the whole manuscript on to a memory stick, and I've already got confirmation from the publishers that they received it on time.' He walked towards Amy and held out his gift. 'This is all I can give you at the moment.'

She took the package and slowly peeled off the Christmas wrapping paper. Inside all the paper was a heavy gold signet ring engraved with Ethan's initials. She looked up at him, puzzled.

'I've had that since I was a boy,' he said. 'My mother and father gave it to me when I was a skinny eighteen-year-old. It started off on my ring finger and then got moved to my little finger. I wore it there for years.' He paused, and she saw the sadness in his eyes. 'Now it won't fit on any of my fingers, but I want it kept safe, and I can't think of anyone else I would trust to do that for me.'

She slipped the band of gold on the third finger of her right hand, where it fitted perfectly. 'I'll take care of it for you.'

Celia gave a little snort. 'It may be solid gold, but it's not worth much. I had all Ethan's old jewellery valued before we got divorced.'

Felix coughed to attract their attention and then held up his hand for silence. 'I haven't given Angela my present yet, and I have to do this right now, in front of everyone, or I'll chicken out again.' He walked over to Angela and pulled her to her feet. 'You called me a coward, and I know I've been a fool, but I hope you haven't completely given up on me.' He took a box out of his pocket. 'I've been carrying this around for almost a year. Like you said, I'm a coward. I've been wasting my life, and yours, and I don't want to do that any more.' He opened the box and took out a diamond ring that sparkled in the light from the fire. 'I'm not going to go down on one knee because I still have my pride, and these are new trousers, but will you marry me, Angela?'

Angela looked at him for a moment, and then put her hands behind her

back. 'This has got to be total commitment, Felix. I love you, but I want you all to myself, and I want your babies, lots of them, before it's too late.'

He reached behind her and pulled her hands round to the front. Holding her against him, he said, 'How many is lots?'

She smiled into his eyes. 'No more than four, I promise.'

'That's a relief.' He took her hand and slipped the ring on her finger — just as Ethan popped the cork on another bottle of champagne.

Celia, for once, looked genuinely pleased. 'Congratulations, Angela. It's about time.'

The evening passed in a blur for Amy. She remembered helping dish up the dinner, and clearing the table afterwards. She remembered hugging Angela and kissing Felix, and wishing them all the happiness in the world, but all she could really think about was Ethan, and the fact that the snow was melting.

He followed her into the kitchen when she went to get some ice from the freezer and, holding her gently by the shoulders, turned her to face him. 'You'll be able to go home tomorrow, if you want to.'

'I know.' She looked into his eyes, hoping he would understand. 'I have to go back to London, Ethan. All this . . . ' she waved a hand, 'happened far too quickly, and we both need time to think.'

He regarded her sombrely. 'I don't need time to think. I know exactly how I feel about you. I want you to change that ring to the other hand until I can buy you a proper one. Something with a diamond in it.'

She looked at him in disbelief. 'Are you proposing to me? We've only known one another a few weeks.'

He shrugged, smiling. 'How much more time do you want to waste?'

She felt her heart stop. She wanted desperately to give him the answer he was waiting for, but she knew this

wasn't real. The setting was magical, the house straight out of a fairy tale, and the handsome prince was asking for her hand in marriage. But tomorrow the snow would melt and the dream would be over — and what would happen when they both woke up?

She moved away from him, away from temptation, away from total disaster. 'I can't, Ethan. I can't say yes. I think I love you, but that's not enough, is it? I need to go back to reality, back to my job in London, back to my friends.' She filled the ice bucket and headed for the door. 'And you need time to get your life sorted out.'

She didn't look back, she couldn't, but she knew he hadn't moved. He was still standing in exactly the same place, watching her leave.

10

Amy hovered on the edge of sleep, wondering what had awakened her, wondering if she had ever really been asleep. Thoughts jostled for a place in her head. Ethan, the house, Celia, the children. Even Felix and Angela. Would their relationship work? There was no way of knowing, no way to be certain. No way to be certain of anything.

She slipped out of bed and caught her breath as the cold hit her. Cathy had loaned her a fleecy nightdress with long sleeves, for which she was eternally grateful, but the velvet mules she had brought with her did very little to keep her toes warm.

She opened the bedroom door and walked out on to the landing. The hallway below was dark and quiet, but she was sure she had heard a noise of some sort. She tied her robe tightly

round her and started down the stairs, heading for the kitchen. Not voices, but little rattles and bangs. Someone trying to be quiet. She pushed open the door and Angela nearly jumped out of her skin.

'Don't go creeping about like that, Amy. You nearly gave me a heart attack.'

'Sorry.' Amy was pleased to find the room still warm. 'What are you doing down here.'

'Making hot chocolate. Want some?'

Amy nodded. 'Someone else who couldn't sleep?

'I've got an excuse,' Angela filled another mug with milk and popped it into the microwave. 'I got proposed to today.'

Amy took a deep breath. 'So did I.'

For a moment Angela stood quite still, just looking at Amy. Then her face broke into a big smile. 'Ethan? He proposed to you? Oh, I'm so pleased. You make him happy, Amy. You'll be great together.' When Amy didn't say anything, her smile faded. 'You did say

yes, didn't you?'

Amy shook her head. She could feel stupid tears pooling in her eyes. 'I wanted to, but I couldn't. We've only just met. We don't know one another.'

Angela put an arm round her shoulders. 'You have the rest of your lives to get to know one another,' she said gently. 'Do you love him?'

'Yes,' Amy suddenly realised there was no doubt in her mind any more. 'I think I'm just scared. I've been single a long time and I don't know if I can live with anyone for the rest of my life.'

The microwave beeped, and Angela laughed. 'Then how about taking one day at a time and see how it goes? Have a long engagement and enjoy getting to know one another.' She stirred chocolate powder into the hot milk. 'I'll get the mince pies out of the fridge and we'll have a midnight feast.'

'Can I join in?' Cathy said from the doorway.

Both women turned and smiled at her. 'We must look like a witches'

coven,' Angela said, 'making spells over the microwave. Make your own hot chocolate, Cathy. We're celebrating a double engagement.'

'A double . . . ' Cathy's eyes opened wide as she looked at Amy's flushed face. 'You and Ethan? Oh, wow!'

'Don't get too excited.' Angela took pies out of the fridge and put them on a plate. 'She hasn't said yes, yet.'

Cathy filled a mug with milk. 'You'll break his heart if you say no, but only say yes if you really love him.'

'I do,' Amy said, turning as the door opened and Celia walked in. Now it really is a witches' coven, she thought to herself.

'You should close the door if you want a secret feast,' Celia said. 'I could hear you upstairs — and I've been listening outside for a while.' She looked at Amy reproachfully. 'I knew there was someone else, but I never guessed it was you. You're a crafty little thing, aren't you? Worming your way in with the children and doing your best

to make me look like a rotten mother.'

Amy sighed. 'It wasn't like that, Celia. I didn't intend falling in love with your ex-husband, and I have no intention of taking your children away from you, but you're not married to Ethan any more. He can do what he likes.'

'I'll go along with that,' Angela said. 'Stop being such a bitch, Celia, and try to enjoy life. You can have the best of both worlds. Ethan will have the children most of the time, but if you want to see them, or take them away on holiday or something, I'm sure he won't stop you.' She handed Celia a plate for her mince pie. 'Look on the bright side. If Amy marries Ethan, she'll have to live here in this cold house and look after your children for you. How's that for punishment?'

Celia tried a smile. 'I don't mean to be a bitch.'

'No, we know that,' Cathy agreed. 'I think it just comes naturally to you.'

Ethan and Felix arrived in the

kitchen just as Angela was heating another plate of mince pies.

'A party, and we weren't invited.' Felix shook his head. 'I'm devastated.'

'There's cake,' Ethan said, 'when you run out of mince pies.'

Amy looked at him, trying to read his face. 'Can I talk to you?' she asked. 'In the drawing room.'

He followed her without a word and she shut the door behind them, feeling her heart start to race. The embers of the fire still glowed in the hearth and the room was warm and cosy. She was quiet for a moment, trying to find the right words, and then she gave up. She might as well just tell the truth. 'I love you Ethan,' she said, looking deep into his eyes. 'I think I fell in love with you the first time you smiled at me, and I want to make you smile a lot more.' Her voice trembled. 'So will you ask me again, please?'

He studied her seriously. 'I thought you wanted to wait. You said you weren't ready.'

She walked over to him and slid her arms round his neck. 'Don't argue with me, Ethan, just ask me again?'

He laughed, a great whoop of delight, and swung her up into the air. 'Amy Franklin, will you marry me?'

She laughed with him. 'Yes, yes, yes, but a long engagement. We have to get to know one another.'

He grinned at her. 'That should be fun.'

She turned in his arms, feeling them close warmly around her. 'It would be silly, wouldn't it?' she murmured against his mouth. 'Me going back to London when we could be together.'

'A complete waste of time.'

His kiss was long and deep, and Amy realised with absolute certainty that there wasn't any other place she wanted to be. At that moment she could quite happily have stayed in his arms forever.

'I see the talking is over,' Celia said from the doorway. 'If it isn't too much trouble, Ethan, I'd like a moment of your time, as well.'

Ethan looked at his watch. 'It's two o'clock in the morning, Celia. Can't this wait?'

Celia shook her head. 'I'll agree to give you full custody of the children as long as I can spend time with them. I'm still their mother, even if I'm not very good at it. And I apologise for trying to sabotage your book. I just wanted to get my own back for the divorce. You made me feel I'd failed as a wife and a mother, and you know I don't like failing at anything.'

She stood up and walked to the door. 'Don't forget to invite me to the wedding.'

⋆ ⋆ ⋆

The next day Amy stood at the front door watching the children load their presents into Felix's big Mercedes. Ethan put his arm round her shoulders and she leant her head against his chest. Tomorrow she would look at plans for a traditional country kitchen.

Celia kissed Ethan primly on the cheek. 'I'm sure you know how to organise everything with the court, and if I don't have to pay for a nanny, I can manage on my present allowance for the time being. I'll tell my solicitor I have too much work to be able to look after the children properly. I don't want anyone to think I'm a bad mother.'

'Thank you, Celia,' Ethan said gratefully. 'You won't regret it.'

'I know I won't.' She looked at Amy thoughtfully. 'You're a lot smarter than I thought you were, and I don't usually underestimate people. Just remember, before you get in too deep to back out, Ethan is a very difficult man to live with.' She smiled without warmth. 'But that's not my problem any more, is it?'

She hurried to the car and slid into the front seat next to Felix, while the children rushed back to the house to say goodbye to their father.

Molly wrapped her arms around Amy. 'I want you to come with us.'

'I can't right now, sweetheart. But

I'm going to miss you lots.'

George looked as if he was near to tears as he hugged his father. 'You promised, dad. You said I could live here with you.'

'And I always keep my promises. You're only going back to London while your mother and I sort things out with the court. Then you're both coming back here for good.'

George squeezed back his tears and looked at Amy. 'Will you be here when we come back?'

She turned to Ethan and looked deep into his warm brown eyes.

'Of course I'll be here,' she said. 'Where else would I be?

THE END

We do hope that you have enjoyed reading this large print book.

Did you know that all of our titles are available for purchase?

We publish a wide range of high quality large print books including:
Romances, Mysteries, Classics
General Fiction
Non Fiction and Westerns

Special interest titles available in large print are:
The Little Oxford Dictionary
Music Book, Song Book
Hymn Book, Service Book

Also available from us courtesy of Oxford University Press:
Young Readers' Dictionary
(large print edition)
Young Readers' Thesaurus
(large print edition)

For further information or a free brochure, please contact us at:
Ulverscroft Large Print Books Ltd.,
The Green, Bradgate Road, Anstey,
Leicester, LE7 7FU, England.
Tel: (00 44) **0116 236 4325**
Fax: (00 44) **0116 234 0205**

THE HOUSE ON THE SHORE

Toni Anders

Roderick Landry, a war artist suffering the after-effects of the trenches, stays for a few weeks at the Cornish hotel where Elvina Simmons lives with her aunts Susie and Tilly. Initially reserved, Roderick eventually warms to Elvina and to life in the sleepy little seaside village. And when, together, they renovate the ruined house on the shore, it seems that their friendship may deepen — to love.

JUST IN TIME FOR CHRISTMAS

Moyra Tarling

Vienna was just a girl when she came to live with Tobias Sheridan and his son, Drew. But when a bitter family feud sent Drew packing, he'd left town, unaware of Vienna's secret passion for him . . . Now he was back. A widower, Drew had returned for the holidays with the grandson his father had never known. But when he took the lovely, grown-up Vienna in his arms, he knew he'd come home at last — just in time for Christmas.

THE SECRET OF HELENA'S BAY

Sally Quilford

Shelley Freeman travels to an idyllic Greek isle to recover from a broken romance. When elderly Stefan von Mueller disappears soon after speaking to her, she's drawn into a disturbing mystery. Everyone else at the resort, including handsome owner Paris Georgiadis, claims never to have seen Stefan. Shelley starts questioning her sanity, and then fearing for her life, as wartime secrets start to unfold. She soon wonders if she can trust Paris with her heart — and with her life . . .

VERA'S VALOUR

Anne Holman

Vera's life, as a wartime bride and British Restaurant cook, is thrown into turmoil when she is handed a vitally important message for her Royal Engineer husband — just after he has departed for D-Day preparations. She eventually catches up with him, but danger is all around them and she must find her own way home again, leaving Geoff to his duties — and without having given him an important message of her own . . .

AN ACT OF LOVE

Margaret Mounsdon

A diamond brooch is the only clue Abbie Rogers has to her own identity . . . and her quest to find her real mother leads her to glamorous actress Diana LaTrobe and the exotic Foxton family. Unaware of the mystery behind Abbie's past, Diana asks Abbie to stay and help her write her memoirs. Amongst the memorabilia Abbie finds the answers to some of her questions, and the reason why she must not fall in love with Diana's son Sim . . .

WAITING FOR A STAR TO FALL

Wendy Kremer

Lucy and Ethan grew up together. Lucy worshipped Ethan from afar and was disenchanted when he left for university, and didn't return. She hadn't realised that this was because of his family's hidden problems. Lucy is now the village librarian and Ethan is a well-known author. When Ethan comes back to the village and into her life again, can he shed his obsession with the past? Will they master the obstacles and find each other before it's too late?

D1382013